THE
Tempt Me
SERIES

Tempting
HEAT

SARA WHITNEY

Tempting Heat

Tempt Me Book 1

Copyright © Sara Whitney 2019

Published by LoveSpark Press, Peoria, IL 61603

This book is a work of fiction. Names, characters, places, and incidents are either products of the author's imagination or used fictitiously. Any resemblance to actual events, locales, or persons, living or dead, is entirely coincidental.

All rights reserved. No part of this publication can be reproduced or transmitted in any form or by any means, electronic or mechanical, without permission in writing from the author or publisher.

Cover art: Deranged Doctor Designs
Editor: Victory Editing

First Edition: November 2019

ISBN: 978-1-953565-00-6

To Jason,
who never gave up when I was the one who got away.
Sorry there's no kick-punching.

And to Mom,
my best cheerleader and my favorite person.

**He knew his luck was bad,
but this is getting ridiculous.**

Tom Castle spent years in love with his best friend's girl. Not that uncommon, really. They even write songs about it. Then she blamed him for her ugly breakup with his now-former friend, and they parted as enemies. *Suuuper* awkward, then, when a blizzard shuts down all of Chicago and Tom ends up stranded with the woman he never expected to see again, more beautiful than ever and still too angry to look him in the eye.

Although Finn Carey's tempted to let Tom take his chances on the streets, she doesn't actually want someone to die in a snowbank—not even the man who hurt her so badly years ago. But her attempts to ignore him and all the complicated feelings he stirs up are foiled when the power goes out in her tiny apartment.

Turns out it's impossible to keep secrets from somebody whose shared body heat is helping you stay alive. Can Tom thaw Finn's chilly exterior before the blizzard stops raging, or is she too stubborn to let go of the ice protecting her heart?

Keep in touch!

Subscribe to Sara's newsletter to stay up on
new releases, sales, and giveaways!
sarawhitney.com/newsletter

CONTENTS

Chapter 1	1
Chapter 2	7
Chapter 3	15
Chapter 4	23
Chapter 5	31
Chapter 6	37
Chapter 7	43
Chapter 8	53
Chapter 9	63
Chapter 10	69
Chapter 11	75
Chapter 12	81
Chapter 13	87
Chapter 14	93
Chapter 15	99
Chapter 16	107
Epilogue	113
Author's Note	119
Also by Sara Whitney	121
About the Author	123

ONE

Finn Carey sagged against the door she'd just wrestled shut and let the overloaded shopping bags fall to her feet so she could fetch the phone buzzing in her pocket. She winced when she saw the face on the screen and took a steadying breath before answering.

"Hi, Mom. I just walked in the door."

"Oh, thank God work let you out early. I hear it's getting terrible out there, and it's barely noon." Halfway through the rush of words, her mother muted the Weather Channel report that had been blaring away in the background, although it didn't silence the concern in her voice. "Was it bad out? Did you run into any trouble?"

"Not too bad and no trouble." Finn pulled off her knit hat to dislodge the layer of snow that had settled there. In truth, it *was* terrible out, but she didn't need to alarm her already overprotective mother.

"Do you have enough supplies to get you through the weekend if it gets worse? And warm clothes if you have to go out?"

"Please don't worry, Mom. I'm safe inside and not

going anywhere." Even if she wanted to, the snow and wind had picked up so fiercely during her commute that she likely wouldn't make it far if she ventured outside right now.

"Oh, I wish you'd move closer to me, Fiona." Her mom barreled on as if Finn hadn't spoken, launching into her favorite refrain. "Are you *sure* you don't want to find a job downstate? I worry about you every day, all alone in Chicago. What if—"

"Alone? Jake lives four miles from me." Finn kept her voice pleasant. It took effort.

"Oh, well, that's different. Your brother's so self-sufficient."

As if Finn were any less self-sufficient than Jake. Both of Shannon Carey's children were methodical and organized, but Jake was older and male, which apparently made him impervious to blowing snow.

"I appreciate your concern, Mom, but you know I love living in Chicago." She cradled the phone against her cheek to shrug out of her coat and hang it on the coatrack, then leaned against the door to kick off her snow-caked boots.

"But what if somebody breaks into your apartment and the police can't get there because of the blizzard?"

She means well. She means well. She means well. Unfortunately, Finn's usual Mom mantra wasn't helping today. "Nobody's breaking into my apartment." She did her best to hide the exasperation she felt, but in the interest of self-sufficiency, it was time for her to end this call. "I gotta go. Please don't worry about me, Mom. I love you. Bye!"

She disconnected and exhaled a steady stream of air, counting slowly in her head until the vein in her temple stopped throbbing. In truth, Finn was far more likely to be smothered by motherly concern than by one of the snowbanks already drifting waist-high against her apartment building.

A gust of wind rattled the living room windows, reminding her of the long, cold weekend she was facing in an apartment already prone to draftiness. Spying a note from her roommate on the kitchen table, she amended that assessment: a long, cold, *lonely* weekend in a drafty apartment.

Hey, sexy thang, Josie had written. *Got called away on a last-minute work trip. Call me! XO*

Finn cocked her head as she reread the note, which ended with Josie's number scrawled at the bottom. Weird that her roommate had jotted down a number that Finn texted daily, but maybe she'd been in such a rush to beat the blizzard that she hadn't been thinking straight. What a bummer too; it ruined Finn's plan for them to use this snowed-in Thursday as an excuse for nothing but wine and binge-watching.

She shot off a quick text to Josie wishing her safe travels to her mystery destination, then turned to the bags she'd lugged home through the increasingly blustery snow. She conducted a quick inventory as she put away the groceries and determined that she had enough to sustain herself for several blizzards. Now all she needed to do was get into some loungewear and prepare herself for an afternoon of assuring Netflix that yes, she was still watching.

She walked past Josie's closed bedroom door to her own room where she shucked her dress pants, silk blouse, and blazer and pulled on her robe to make the quick trip down the hall to the bathroom. A shower might help thaw out the icicles in her blood.

One luxurious sudsing later, she was toweled off and swathed in leggings, her softest T-shirt, and a fuzzy cardigan. She was braiding her wet black hair when her phone buzzed with a call from Josie.

"Hey, Finnie! You made it home okay?" An echoing clamor of voices in the background almost drowned out Josie's words.

Finn headed toward the kitchen to get dinner started. "No problems except fighting the ravenous crowd for milk, bread, and eggs. Where are you?"

"Gotta defend those french toast supplies," Josie laughed. "I'm temporarily stranded at the Denver airport on the way to Las Vegas."

"Vegas, huh?" Finn paused in the middle of pulling spices down from the cabinet.

"Yep. The blizzard trapped Gil in Ontario, which means he can't give the company presentation at the marketing association trade show on Saturday. He called this morning and gave me fifteen minutes to pack and haul ass to O'Hare to beat the snow."

Fifteen minutes was laughably short for a clotheshorse like Josie; no wonder she'd been distracted while leaving the note.

"Sounds rough. I didn't even hear you come in last night." Finn stood on her tiptoes to grab the chili powder from the top shelf. "Was O'Hare a zoo?"

"*Bananas*. But I used my gentle persuasion on a few airline employees who managed to squeeze me onto the flights I needed."

Finn grinned at the thought of her not-at-all-shy roommate steamrolling every employee who got in the way. "Well, enjoy Sin City, but know that I'm planning to drink all the wine I brought home to share."

Josie gave an appreciative smack of her lips that was interrupted by the squawk of an intercom announcement. "Oh, that's my flight! Better make sure they don't give my seat away. Love you, byeeeee!"

Leave it to Josie to be bouncy in the middle of an airport hellscape. Shaking her head, Finn flipped on the radio so the increasingly dire weather reports could keep her company during dinner prep. She'd dumped the last of the ingredients into the slow cooker when something scuffed on the kitchen tile behind her.

"Josie?"

Finn whirled around to see a disheveled brown-haired man standing six feet away, and as she opened her mouth to shriek, one thought floated through her mind: *Mom's going to carve "I told you so" on my tombstone.*

TWO

Tom Castle had woken up disoriented and hungover as hell, and the screaming woman wasn't helping. He squinted in the bright light of the kitchen, so harsh compared to the dark cave he'd just left, and addressed the blur in front of him.

"Whoa, sorry, I didn't mean to startle you."

As his eyes adjusted, he realized the blur was short, skinny, and brandishing a knife in his direction. He took two quick steps back.

"You're not Josie."

"No!"

He held his hands out in front of him in what he hoped was a soothing gesture and kept his voice calm and even. "Okay, listen, this is a misunderstanding. I just woke up, but give me a second, and I'll get out of—"

"*Tom Castle?*"

If anything, the blur sounded even more hostile. But this time the hostility sounded... familiar. He risked a shuffle step forward and forced his bloodshot eyes to focus on the woman in front of him.

"Huckleberry?" he asked in amazement.

Huckleberry Finn. His lips shaped the old nickname without conscious thought, but the reminder of their high school American lit class did nothing to relax her guard. Instead, she spun around to grab a second knife with her free hand.

"What the fuck, Tom? Why are you in my apartment?"

Holy shit, Finn Carey was finally going to finish the job she'd wanted to do since the end of their senior year. They'd be finding pieces of him all over Cook County when the thaw hit.

Then his brain lurched to life and jangled a warning about how this must look to her. "Hey, I'm really sorry I scared you. I had no idea..." He cast his eyes around the small apartment, looking for any clues he'd missed the night before. Come to think of it, it *was* oppressively tidy enough to belong to an uptight control freak like Finn. "Josie's your roommate, I take it?"

Comprehension dawned, and the fear on Finn's face twisted into the narrow-eyed loathing he remembered from eight years ago. At least she set the edged weapons back on the counter. "And you're one of Josie's hookups."

Even though she hadn't asked a question, he scrubbed a hand down his face and answered anyway. "No, I'm not." After a lifetime of shitty luck, he'd come to expect the worst, but ending up in Finn Carey's apartment by pure happenstance might be the biggest fuck-you Fate had ever dealt him. "I walked her home from the bar last night. That's it."

She scoffed. "Oh, so you 'chivalrously'"—Tom felt as though her air quotes were unnecessarily sarcastic—"escorted my drunk roommate home and, with no ulterior motives, ended up sleeping in her bed for hours and hours after she packed a bag and left the apartment that I happen to share with her?"

Even though it did all sound ridiculous, an echo of that old hurt roared to life in his chest. *Of fucking course* she didn't trust that he had good intentions.

"That's exactly what happened," he snapped. "I passed out and woke up just now with my virtue intact."

"So you had no idea she and I live together? This is all some cosmic coincidence?"

God, he was too undercaffeinated for this. "Don't flatter yourself, Huck. I haven't exactly been monitoring your whereabouts since high school." True, mostly. "I was trying to be a good guy last night and apparently picked the wrong person to do it with."

The skepticism on her face tipped his own hurt into anger, and he was suddenly desperate to leave before it morphed into sadness. He'd had enough of that already when it came to her. "Well, this has been fun. Give me five minutes and I'll get out of your life." Again.

Finn laughed. It wasn't a nice laugh. "Good luck with that."

She pointed to the windows, and he crossed the room to pull back a curtain.

"Shit," he breathed. The snow they'd been predicting yesterday had hit hard. The street between the tall apartment buildings lining the block was untouched by a plow, and the sidewalks weren't any better. The cars parked in front were little more than fluffy white mounds. Just his luck to heinously oversleep on the one day the meteorologists' dire predictions didn't turn out to be exaggerations.

"I just need to get home from... wherever we are. Any chance this is near Evanston?" He was grasping at straws, praying to the god of deeply unlucky graduate students that he'd somehow ended up miraculously close to his apartment.

Finn's pretty face twisted into a sneer. "How do you not know where we are?"

"A little whiskey on top of a lot of sleep deprivation isn't great for short-term memory," he snapped, patience gone. She rolled her eyes, and like that it was eight years ago and he was sitting across from her in the cafeteria, drinking in every nuance of her expressive face.

"We're in River North." She spoke with exaggeratedly slow enunciation, as if he were too dim to understand the geography of the city he'd grown up in.

But the map of Chicago was inscribed on his brain, and Tom's tiny bubble of hope popped. He was fit, but he wasn't about to attempt a twenty-mile walk in this weather. He clenched his hands in frustration, trying to think.

"So I'll get an Uber. Or a taxi." But another peek out the window told him that was futile. Anything available would be in high demand, and none would be able to make it onto this snow-entombed street anyway. "Fuck. Okay then, where's the nearest L station?"

That unamused laugh again. "It's seven blocks away. I barely made it home ninety minutes ago, and the snow's gotten worse since then."

He stared at the patch of yellow linoleum stretching between them while he considered his options. On one hand was a long walk to the train in a blizzard. On the other hand was Finn's icy, narrowed gaze.

Blizzard it was. He wasn't sure he could survive another second of her obvious displeasure in his company.

"I'll grab my things and get out of your way."

Finn's brows snapped together, but she didn't say anything when he turned on his heel and ducked back into the room from whence he'd emerged. He cast one longing glance at the warm-looking bed with its enticingly tossed-back covers before sliding on his shoes and coat and slinging his bag over his shoulder. When he emerged, Finn had moved the knives to the sink, apparently deciding he was no longer a threat now that he was headed to his death on the snowy streets of Chicago.

"I think that note is for you." She gestured at a sheet of paper on the table.

He glanced at it but left it where it was. Even if he was interested in spending more time with Josie, he'd never pocket another woman's number in front of Finn. "Okay. I'll... Well, I'll see you never." He zipped his coat to his chin and prayed it was up to the task. "Enjoy your blizzard."

She offered him a tight smile. "Turn right when you leave the building. Two blocks, then go left another block, then right and it's a straight shot."

"Thanks." Then he cut their excruciating encounter short by exiting the apartment and clattering down three flights of stairs to the black-and-white-tiled lobby. He tugged on his hat and gloves, then took a deep breath and pushed the exterior door open.

At first nothing happened. The door wouldn't budge. He put his shoulder into it and gave it a good shove, feet slipping on the tile as he strained to find leverage. Slowly the door inched open, pushing against the mound of snow that had already drifted against it and unleashing a blast of arctic air across his face. When he'd cleared a wide-enough arc, he slipped through and sank up to his knees in the thick, fluffy stuff covering the sidewalk.

Fuck. The cold and wet immediately seeped into his jeans, socks, and shoes. How was there this much snow already? When he and Josie had made it to her apartment at close to four in the morning, it had only been spitting.

A fierce gust of wind whapped him full in the face then, spraying snow against the apartment and adding to the already enormous drifts.

He took a moment to get oriented and set out in what he hoped was the right direction, but after making it only a few feet, he found himself laboring to draw breath into his lungs. The heavy snow was almost impossible to move through, and he wasn't sure he'd physically be able to make it the L station before succumbing to frostbite or exhaustion.

Fear cut through him, sharper than the wind, but he plowed ahead, pushing through the untouched snow. It crept under his coat sleeves, and the flakes landing on his cheeks and nose melted and trickled down his overheated face to pool inside his collar. The street itself was silent save the howling of the wind and his own labored breaths, and his blue puffer jacket was the only spot of color in this otherwise white, swirling world.

God, how long was this block? How close was he to the corner? How long would it take to reach the next street if he had to fight through drifts the whole way?

"Tom! Hey, Tom!"

At first, he thought he was imagining the faint sound of his name being tossed on the wind, but when it persisted, he forced himself to pause and search for the source. A dark shape leaned out of an upper window, partially obscured by the thick flakes in the air. It was Finn, her long braid a stiff banner in the wind as she shouted like a fairy-tale princess in a tower at the peasants on the street below.

"Come back up! I can't let you die in a snowbank." She pulled her head in, then popped it right back out. "Even if you deserve it!"

Make that a *mean* fairy-tale princess.

For a tenth of a second, Tom thought about waving her off and continuing on to the train, but that was obviously insane. His teeth were already chattering, and he hadn't even cleared the end of her block yet. He'd changed his mind; dying of exposure was only slightly less preferable than returning to Finn's apartment.

"Okay!" he hollered back, pivoting to follow the tracks he'd just made. Incredibly, they were already starting to fill in.

When he reached the door, she buzzed him in, and he wrestled the heavy beast back open, practically throwing himself to the tiles in gratitude that he was safe from the elements. He took a minute to catch his breath before dragging himself back up the stairs.

Her apartment door was ajar, and he rapped once before walking in and nudging it shut behind him.

She perched on one of the kitchen chairs, spine stiff. "There's no way you were going to make it eight blocks."

Tom leaned against the door and tried not to shiver at the sensation of wet denim clinging to his cold flesh. "No. Not likely," he admitted, unable to stop the tremor that rolled through him as his icy socks squelched in his shoes.

Her mouth flattened. "Then I guess we'll have to do our best to ignore each other until things clear up."

He nodded, although it was more like uncoordinated jerking as his extremities tried to shut down from the cold. "Good thing we've had plenty of practice at that." Her nostrils flared, but he was too frozen to celebrate landing a jab. "Listen, I know we haven't spoken since... everything went down. But you've got my word that I haven't turned into a murderer or an arsonist or a vegan or anything weird. I'm just a guy who overslept in a strange apartment on the worst possible day."

She sighed and stood up, gesturing to the coatrack behind him. "Hang your coat up. I'm guessing you'd like a hot shower?"

He almost let out a sob. "Yes. That would be amazing." He'd deal with his sodden clothes later. Right now he wanted to be enveloped by hot, steamy water.

She pointed to the bathroom. "If you give me a second, I'll find you some clean towels."

She might have allowed him back into her apartment, but her voice was as cold as the wind that had buffeted him outside. He didn't care though; he was already moving across the small living room, hoping he'd be able to feel his toes again soon.

THREE

Finn heard the shower start up as she was raiding the linen closet and felt a spurt of annoyance. Her unwelcome guest hadn't followed her instructions to wait until she'd handed him a towel and retreated to a safe distance.

Tom Castle. In her home. In her *shower*. Their last real conversation all those years ago had been a screaming match—well, she'd screamed; he'd remained pale and silent—and now he was naked in the next room. *And* he'd had the audacity to get even better-looking in the intervening years.

While she was mentally reconciling the skinny teenager she'd known with the broad-shouldered specimen of today, an idea struck her. She might not be happy with this situation, but her mother had raised her to be hospitable. She rummaged through a basket in the back of her closet until she hit pay dirt and, arms full, approached the bathroom door, which Tom had left cracked open. Taking a deep breath, she knocked hard once.

"I've got towels." She tried to sound calm and assertive, as if she brought terry cloth to naked men every day. Dammit, Josie wouldn't blink an eye at this; her roommate was so much better at rolling with the unexpected than Finn was.

His disembodied voice floated from the shower. "Come on in. Drop them wherever."

She could push the whole bundle through the cracked door without ever entering. In fact, that's obviously what she *should* do. And yet that was her hand reaching out and nudging the door open, and those were her feet carrying her into the steamy room, the bundle of fabric clutched to her chest. After all, she'd be in and out fast, and Tom would stay safely behind the shower curtain.

The mostly clear shower curtain with only a small spray of daisies on it.

Oh God.

That dark curly hair, the long torso, those glorious cheekbones. All of it wet and only a few feet away. She swallowed hard and deposited the folded stack onto the closed laundry hamper next to the sink, intending to leave immediately until her eyes snagged on the tall shape standing under the spray. His palms were flat against the shower wall, and his head was tipped forward. She'd bet he was reveling in the warmth after his time outside, closing his amber-colored eyes against the spray as it slid down the muscles of his back to travel downward—

Aaaaand she'd turned into a creeper.

"I left stuff next to the sink," she yelled, then slipped out of the bathroom, hoping like hell he hadn't noticed her loitering.

The rest of the apartment felt even chillier after the humid bathroom. She pulled an afghan off the back of the couch and wrapped herself in it before sinking onto the cushions. She should've let his worthless ass fall into a snowdrift and be carried away by a snowplow. He deserved it.

Except she'd felt an actual bolt of fear race through her as she'd watched his slow progress in front of her building and thought about him fighting like that for blocks and blocks. For once in her orderly life, she'd acted impulsively, and now she had to figure out what to do with him. Well, not *do* with him, obviously, but would it be possible for them to ignore each other for the next twenty-four hours—or, God forbid, longer?

"I need you to stop throwing this hissy fit, Mama Nature," she muttered to the slice of gray sky visible through the windows. After a moment's deliberation, she texted a quick rundown of her situation to big brother Jake. Knowing his busy schedule, he'd only think to check it if she'd been missing for a week, but it was still preferable to keep him in the loop rather than her panic-first-ask-questions-later mom. That done, she let the phone fall to her lap as her oh-so-helpful brain conjured images of what might be happening behind that closed bathroom door.

When the shower shut off, she lunged for one of the magazines sitting on the coffee table so it wouldn't look like she'd been staring into space, thinking about him. Which, of course, was exactly what she'd been doing. She flipped randomly to an article about personal finance for single women but couldn't stop herself from looking up when the door opened and her houseguest emerged, his cheeks flushed pink from the heat of the shower.

"I don't know what kind of witchcraft it took for you to find things that fit me, but I'm grateful," he said. "I would've worn sparkly pink tights if it meant not putting those wet jeans back on."

Her eyes ran down his body. He *was* talking about the clothes adorning his person, after all; she was only participating in the conversation. The long-sleeved DePaul T-shirt stretched across his well-muscled chest, and the black track pants were a touch too short, which made the fuzzy socks he was wearing stand out even more.

She looked down to hide a smile. "My friend's gym is nearby, and he sometimes comes here to change before or to clean up afterward. We keep a little supply of things for him that he's left over the years."

Tom kicked up one foot to contemplate the lime-green and cotton-candy-pink stripes on his socks.

"Okay, not those," she amended. "Those are mine. They're the warmest socks I own. I thought you'd appreciate them after your brush with death."

He offered her a crooked grin, and her breath caught in her throat. She hadn't seen that smile in so long. She'd missed that smile, despite it all. He still had those dimples on either side of his wide mouth, so deep a woman could fall in if she wasn't careful.

Good thing she knew to be careful.

"That was thoughtful. Thanks." He seated himself in the overstuffed chair next to the couch and stretched out his legs, hooking one ankle over the other on the ottoman. His smile faded as he pushed his dark wet hair back from his forehead. "So. Do I need to sleep with one eye open, or should we talk about th—"

"*No*." The word burst from her throat, and she rolled the magazine until her knuckles were white and she was able to speak calmly. "No. What's the point? Let's just try to ignore each other until you can leave."

She offered him her best tough-girl face, and he simply nodded and looked down at those ridiculous socks. A particularly strong gust of wind rattled the windows in their panes, and Finn shivered. What a catastrophe. With or without Josie, she'd been counting on a chill weekend. But no way was she going to let her guard down for a second with Tom there, both familiar and strange and stirring up all kinds of long-buried emotions.

So she lied. "I actually have a big work project that I brought home with me. I'll set up in my room." It was the only activity she could think of that would give her an excuse to shut her door and pretend that Tom had remained a painful memory from her past. "What about you?"

He jiggled his knee, and she wondered if he was uneasy too or just burning off excess energy.

"I've always got a mountain of work I can do." He pointed to his bag near the door. "Have laptop, will travel."

"Kitchen table okay for you?"

"Sure." He surged to his feet, and wow, she'd forgotten how tall he was and how tiny he made her feel.

She shrugged off the afghan and stood too, the forgotten magazine slithering to the floor. "Sure," she repeated. "There's soda and beer in the fridge. Help yourself to whatever."

Tom crossed the room to grab his bag and dropped it on the table. "Thanks. Can I keep any spare change I find when I rummage through your drawers?"

"Ha," she said flatly.

He offered her another lopsided grin. "Now that I think about it, it's probably not worth the trouble. I've got a teaching assistant's stipend that keeps me in the lifestyle to which I've lowered my standards. Spare change isn't going to make a dent in the student loans." He pulled a power cord out of his bag and swiveled his head around the room.

She pointed at the outlet along the kitchen wall, then asked in spite of herself. "Teaching assistant?"

He plugged in and returned to the table. "I'm a PhD candidate in economics at Northwestern."

His hair was drying into those familiar curls, *and* he was reminding her of just how smart he was? Unfair.

"Makes sense. You were the only one in econ class who actually enjoyed learning about *The Wealth of Nations*."

He grinned at her over the top of his MacBook. "Would you believe that's what my dissertation's on? I'm examining its compatibility with the rise in ethical investment portfolios."

A memory surfaced of his enthusiasm for the topic, so at odds with the other bored-out-of-their-minds students in class. "I bet your grad school study groups aren't nearly as much fun as we were."

His smile faded. "They aren't."

Well, hell. Why had she brought that up? Their high school study group had been her, Tom, and Dylan—her boyfriend and Tom's best friend—and they'd been a happy little trio. Until they weren't. Judging by the look on his face, it wasn't a particularly pleasant memory for him either. Time to shut this down.

"I'll be in there." She hitched a thumb over her shoulder toward her room. "Holler if you need anything."

Before she'd gone three steps, his voice stopped her. "Hey, Huck?"

She turned slowly, apprehension and anticipation at war in her stomach.

"Wi-Fi password?"

Ah. Of course. He wanted to get online. She rattled it off and fled to her bedroom, where everything was neat and tidy and not covered in a sticky layer of emotions.

FOUR

Tom had prepared a speech once upon a time. A furious defense to show Finn Carey exactly how wrong she was about him. He'd imagined himself delivering it in a variety of settings: in the hallway between classes, at a cafeteria table, from the stage at graduation. It never happened, of course, but each time the crux of his message would've been the same: *How could you ever think I would do that?*

He'd never imagined delivering it almost a decade later in the apartment of Finn Carey, adult. Yet the arguments he'd gone over and over in his head came rushing back, ready to unleash, as she'd sat on the couch, trying to hide behind a magazine. He'd even given her an opening.

She didn't want to talk about it? Fine. He'd ignore their history and count the minutes until he could get the fuck back out of her life. Good thing he had two hundred pages of dissertation edits to plow through.

He pulled one of the binders from his bag and smoothed his fingers over the printed sheets of his rough draft, imagining he could feel the power of Adam Smith's economic theories vibrating on the page. With his earbuds plugged in and the pages spread on the table in front of him, he soon forgot all about the uncomfortable kitchen chair, the chilliness in the apartment, the storm howling outside, even the woman in the next room.

Three hours later, he rested his elbows on the table and sank his fingers into his overlong hair as he stared at the note on page 108. Professorial handwriting was erratic on a good day, and with the addition of a stain of some kind, probably coffee, it was downright illegible. He gave a growl of frustration.

"Something wrong?"

Tom jumped and yanked out his earbuds, surprised to find Finn hovering at the opposite end of the table, arms stiff at her sides. While he'd been staring at his screen, the rest of the apartment had grown dark beyond the pool of light from the overhead fixture. She stood at the edge of the illumination, her unbraided hair a curtain of midnight around her tense shoulders.

His laidback chill had always acted as a counterweight to her tightly-wound in high school. Assuming things hadn't changed *that* much, he slipped into role of extremely relaxed guy and prayed it would get her to stop moving around the apartment like she was strapped to a board. "Yes, actually. Can you make heads or tails of this?" He pointed out the illegible note, and she moved around the table, her forehead wrinkling as she examined the red ink.

Even in comfy clothes, she looked carefully put together, exactly the way he remembered her. Her family had skirted the poverty line when she was growing up, but she'd always carried herself as if her meticulously cleaned and pressed thrift-store clothing was *haute couture*. And here she was now in an immaculate white sweater and soft, expensive-looking pants, with suede slippers on her feet. Good for her.

"Be sludge turtle Jay?" She squinted at the page. "I don't know anything about graduate-level economics. Does that make any sense to you?"

He shrugged helplessly. "It's the newest member on my dissertation committee. She replaced a professor who stepped away for family reasons last week, and I haven't figured out her handwriting yet."

She glanced at it again. "Oof. Brutal. Is that pretty common?"

"Bad handwriting? Yes. New committee members in the defense stage? Definitely not." Anxiety over the influx state of his dissertation committee reared its head, but Tom shoved it aside and reached for nonchalance. "That's actually my second replacement this semester, out of five. Number one had green card issues, and now number two's in California taking care of her father after he fell and broke his hip, so it's been a lot of catching new people up. My luck strikes again."

"Oh man, the Tom Castle bad luck!" He saw the memories fire in her synapses. "What did you always used to say? 'Expect the worst. Prepare for the worst. It's always the worst'?"

He nodded and tried not to be flattered that she remembered. "I'm still pretty much an optimism-free zone."

"Let's see..." She tipped her head toward the ceiling in thought. "You got a flat tire on prom night and almost missed the dance. Yours was the only flooded locker when the high school roof leaked. Oh, and then there was the ostrich that charged at you and only you during our trip to the Brookfield Zoo."

"That ostrich thought I was a sexy beast." He smirked to cover for the fact that those were minor speed bumps compared to the true disappointments of his life. When you spend years watching your best friend kiss the girl you're crazy about, you start to doubt that things will ever break your way.

Enough of that though. He leaned back in his chair and felt his spine protest. "I've been sitting for too long." He groaned and stretched, and when Finn moved to the countertop and took the lid off the slow cooker sitting there, he choked back a different kind of groan. Now that he'd pulled his mind off research, his hunger came roaring up to meet the spicy smell filling the kitchen.

Seconds later he was standing at her side, using his six-inch height advantage to peer over her head at the concoction she was stirring. "What is it?"

She laughed at the awe in his voice. "It's chili. You did say you weren't a vegan, right?"

"You're willing to share?" The idea hadn't even occurred to him.

She looked up with a frown. "Did you really think I'd let you starve?"

He shrugged and took a step back. "I didn't want to assume, and I don't want to impose." Plus, six hours ago, he'd have bet all the cash in his wallet that if fierce little Finn Carey ever put food in front of him, it'd be poisoned.

She grabbed two blue bowls from the cabinet and picked up a ladle. "If I don't feed you, you'll die of hunger in my living room rather than of exposure in a snowbank fifteen feet from my front door. Both would be my fault, but your dying in my apartment would be way more inconvenient for me. Ergo, I'll share."

What a day. She'd kicked him out, rescued him, warmed him, dressed him, and now was going to feed him. "This is literally saving my life. The last thing I ate was a ham sandwich in the TA lounge yesterday afternoon."

"Then maybe you should've had dinner last night instead of hitting on strange women at bars." She shoved two full bowls into his hands harder than was strictly necessary, and despite her obvious irritation, his stomach growled loudly.

"Apparently so. That's what we researchers call independent confirmation." He returned to the table as she pulled sour cream and shredded cheese out of the fridge and joined him.

"Ha." She accepted the bowl he slid across to her. "It's not fancy, but at least it's warm. If Josie were here..."

Her roommate's name landed like a grenade in the space between them, and discomfort crept along Tom's spine. He leaned forward. "Hey. About that—"

"Yeah, I don't need an explanation." She reached for the sour cream, her eyes locked on the container.

Tom pushed ahead because no way in hell was he letting *this* situation pass without her hearing his side. "Look, Josie and I ended up in the same bar at closing time, and I volunteered to make sure she got home okay. When I'm out, I try to notice if someone looks like they might run into trouble on their own."

Finn's shoulders were tense as she stirred her chili, and Tom sighed, not wanting to wade too close to their uncomfortable history. "Long story short, she insisted I come in because it had started snowing, and then, honestly, I passed out. I'd been up for two days straight grading papers, so those shots of whiskey did me in. It... wasn't my proudest moment." He scrubbed a hand through his hair in embarrassment. The previous night was one big, loud blur in his mind.

Finn cut her eyes up at him, then back down. "I told you, it doesn't matter to me what you guys did."

"What we *didn't* do," he said, anxious to jostle her out of that reserved politeness.

After a beat, she inclined her head in acknowledgment, the movement stiff. "Makes sense. Only someone who'd had a hell of a night wouldn't immediately know I wasn't Josie."

Tom knew a trap when he saw one, so he busied himself adding cheese to his bowl. His memories of Josie from the bar on Wednesday were of a stacked redhead with a big laugh, which was certainly a contrast to the black-haired sylph sitting across from him, her pert nose, pointed chin, and graceful collarbones creating a riot of delicate angles.

He forced a lazy smile and gave an "easy come, easy go" gesture. "Eh, redheads aren't generally my type." He saw the question flit across her face: *What* is *your type these days?* But before she could ask it, before he was tempted to tell her that his type had only ever been petite, sharp-jawed, black-haired women, he took his first bite of chili. He didn't have to fake the moan of appreciation he gave as the spicy-meat-and-tomato goodness exploded on his tongue.

"Oh my God." He all but submerged his head in the bowl in his haste to inhale all its deliciousness, and Finn offered him the first full smile he'd seen from her all day.

"There's plenty more." She gestured to the stove, and

he immediately stood to grab seconds. "You seriously didn't sleep for two days to grade papers?"

He grimaced as he sat back down, although inside he was pleased that she was picking up the conversational ball. "I'm a TA for the Intro to Macro class, and I'd been putting off a mountain of grading, plus I have an editing deadline on my dissertation, which I've *also* been putting off. The perfect storm before the perfect storm." He gestured to the snow that still swirled outside the windows before turning back to his bowl.

"Ah. More bad luck," she said.

That drew another actual smile from her, and he felt a curl of pleasure unfold in his stomach. He was safe and warm and inside, his socks were dry, and Finn Carey was smiling at him like she used to. All in all, it could be a worse blizzard.

Oh, look at that. A sliver of optimism. He decided to chase that rare feeling. "So. I answered your questions. Now you need to answer one for me."

She froze as he set his spoon down and gravely folded his hands together.

"Do you have coffee for the morning, or should I throw myself into a snowbank right now?"

Her lips twitched. "I have coffee. Fresh grind pour-over. Hope that's okay."

Tom picked up his bowl again to dig in. "With this kind of hospitality, Huckleberry, I may never leave."

FIVE

Finn stood at the sink with her hands in soapy water, considering all the ways her day was unraveling. She'd spent the afternoon hiding in her room getting no work done and grappling with the urge to yell at Tom and to hug him and to demand that he tell her all the stories about his life that she'd missed since they'd stopped confiding everything to each other eight years ago. And then he'd sat across from her at dinner, all charming and smiley, and that impulse had grown too dangerous and far too tempting. God, he was the worst, reminding her of all the things she used to like about him. Time to hit the brakes.

"So about tonight. I assume you're good sleeping in Josie's room again?"

She addressed her words to the dishwater, but Tom joined her at the sink, reaching for a towel and starting to dry the dishes she'd set to the side.

"Actually, no. I feel a little weird about it."

That made two of them. But she clamped down on a

wave of irrational jealousy to point out, "You slept there last night."

He took a bowl from her and ran the dishtowel over its clean, dripping surface. "Yeah, but last night I passed out at the foot of the bed on top of the covers, like a dog. And now I'm some random guy she only exchanged a few sentences with who's sleeping in her sheets? It feels wrong. I was thinking I should maybe take the couch."

Her TV-watching couch? In the middle of her living room? Nope. No way was Finn letting that happen. He couldn't sleep out in the open. She didn't want to see what he looked like asleep, didn't want to know whether those full lips parted in relaxation, didn't want to hear his deep, even breaths. Didn't want to picture Tom at rest every time she sat on the couch's overstuffed cushions in the future. Best to keep all that behind Josie's bedroom door.

"Don't be dumb," she told him briskly. "You already slept there once, and we don't have a ton of extra blankets to make a bed on the couch. Josie won't care. She liked you enough to bring you home in the first place."

Was that a blush she saw heating his skin? It was hard to tell in the low lighting.

"I *told* you, nothing happened. We just—"

"Oh my God, will you stop? I said I believe you," she almost shouted.

His whole body vibrated as if someone had struck his breastbone like a gong, and he looked so stricken that she wanted to smooth a hand through his curls and tell him everything was all right. But before she could act on something so foolish, he spun and stalked to the window.

For a moment she wondered if he was thinking about their old fight, but that didn't quite fit. It had never been a matter of truth versus lies or her believing him. It had all been about what he'd done and how much it had hurt her.

Still, he stood like a statue, silhouetted by the muted glow of the streetlights outside, and she felt unaccountably drawn in by his solitude. Unsure if he'd welcome it, she crossed the room to stand next to him. Incredibly, fat flakes were still tumbling across their field of vision.

"I don't think I'll be able to leave tomorrow morning."

"Agreed," she said. "They were predicting another eight to ten inches by Friday morning."

She was standing close enough to feel his body tremble, yet when she turned to face him, it wasn't distress she saw, but suppressed laughter. "What?" He pinched his mouth shut and shook his head, so she turned her full scowl on him. "Seriously, *what?*"

"I've got your eight to ten inches right here, baby," he blurted.

The juvenile remark after his brief melancholy startled a laugh out of her, and he shrugged apologetically. "Sorry, but you set me up."

"I certainly did not! It was a *weather report*." She tried to keep an outraged face while all her swimsuit parts woke up and cracked their knuckles in anticipation. "I swear, you men and your dick jokes."

"We're animals, I know."

He was unrepentant, and she was grateful for it. He was welcome to joke about whatever he wanted as long as it chased away the strange sadness that had poured off him earlier.

He turned his back to the snowy view and leaned against the wall, crossing his arms. His muscles stretched his slightly-too-small shirt, and she'd never been so grateful for Richard's slender build. If he were any more buff, his clothes wouldn't show off every line of Tom's biceps and chest, and wouldn't that have been a tragedy?

Even though she had no claim on Tom, she was immensely relieved that he and Josie hadn't slept together and that he hadn't even followed her gorgeous roommate home hoping for that outcome. How irrational, but there it was, humming underneath her skin.

In high school, Dylan and Tom had been a package deal. Date the quarterback, and spend acres of time with his brainy best friend. Eventually she'd discovered that she and Tom shared a love of puns and dad jokes, and while Dylan spent his time at the gym or traveling to away games with the team, Tom had been the one to listen to stories about her day or to tease her out of her bad moods when school got too overwhelming. And while Tom had turned those big amber eyes on a few of her female classmates over the years, his relationships never lasted long and he always ended up back with her and Dylan, where it felt like he belonged.

She shook her head sharply. Too many memories for one night. She walked back into the kitchen to finish cleaning up, hoping a bout of tidying would banish the restlessness she felt.

"I left an unopened toothbrush on the bathroom counter for you. Any other toiletries, you're going to have to borrow and risk getting girl cooties." She poured the leftover chili into a plastic container, then turned to find him watching her. Oh God, had he noticed that her agitation had ratcheted up over the past few minutes? If so, he didn't let on.

"My needs are simple, but I appreciate the toothbrush. Thank you." He gestured to the slow cooker. "Can I help you with that?"

"No, I got it." She set the insert into the sink to soak, hyperaware of his eyes watching her movements. "So, I, uh, guess I'm headed to bed. Good night. If you need anything, knock."

After one last glance around the kitchen, which was as spotless as it had been predinner, she headed toward her room.

"I will," Tom called after her, and she couldn't decide whether she'd be horrified or thrilled if he actually did.

SIX

In the end, Tom didn't go knocking on Finn's door even though he *did* need an iPhone charger. But she'd looked so uncomfortable at the thought of sleeping with only the tiny bathroom between them that he didn't have the heart to actually tap on that solidly shut door of hers once he realized how low his battery was.

So he'd powered down his phone and tossed and turned in Josie's pink-striped sheets. The next morning he was up early, and the first thing he did was cross to the window to check out the snow situation.

It was still coming down. How was there enough snow in the universe that it was somehow still falling on Chicago?

"Dammit." He rested his forehead on the cold glass. Entire days alone with Finn Carey had literally been one of his teenage wet dreams. Now, it was a grown-up kind of torture.

Finn, Dylan, and Tom. The Beauty, the Brawn, and the Brains. Of course Dylan hadn't given a second thought to leaving Finn in the stands with Tom during football games. In what world did Beauty choose Brains when Brawn was the quarterback and the homecoming king?

But standing by the window right then, all he could hear were Finn's words from the night before: *I said I believe you.* Years too late to undo the damage, and in a wholly different situation, yet it had still taken all his willpower not to demand to know why now but not then? Why hadn't she given him the benefit of the doubt at a time when they were daily confidants, when she'd been the center of his world?

"Roads still not clear?"

Her voice made him jump, and his pulse ratcheted up when she joined him at the window. Yet again, she looked pristine and tailored in jeans and a fitted long-sleeve T-shirt, a walking advertisement for look-but-don't-wrinkle.

"How is there that much snow in the world?" she asked.

"Literally what I was just thinking."

She dropped the curtain and walked to the kitchen where she busied herself getting coffee ready. He joined her and opened cupboards until he found the mug stash and selected two. He needed cool-and-unbothered Tom to report for duty ASAP.

"More editing work for me. I can't waste a Friday even if it's a snow day." He nodded his chin toward the laptop on the kitchen table.

She poured for both of them and added cream to her mug. "Yeah, my boss is expecting my project next week, so I may as well keep going on it."

He declined her offer of coffee additives and leaned against the counter. "So what did our graduating class's worst economics student end up doing with her life?"

"Not accounting, I'll tell you that." Her expression brightened. "I work for QR Marketing. We measure consumer opinions surrounding product launches. Right now I'm finalizing a set of focus group questions for a new fragrance line."

Rigidly organized solicitor of opinions. It fit the Finn he remembered.

"I assume you want to know more than 'smells good' or 'nah'?"

She leveled a look over the rim of her University of Illinois at Chicago mug. "If you mock my profession, I'll douse you with the perfume while you sleep. Between you and me, it reeks."

Tom grinned, delighted that she was teasing him. When she chose to engage, her whole demeanor changed. Her lips pressed together with humor, and her eyes crinkled at the corners. He decided to push his luck. "Want to work out here? Keep me company?"

The crinkles disappeared, replaced with apprehension. Then the line between her eyes relaxed. "Actually, yes. The desk in my room is a little cramped."

After she fetched her work materials, they toiled side by side at the kitchen table for hours, silent but for the click of their fingers on their keyboards and the instrumental alternative Spotify station they'd agreed on. Tom would occasionally glance up to catch a glimpse of her brow furrowed in thought. She'd left her hair loose, and the dark strands fell forward when she shifted closer to her screen. As the afternoon wore on, he found himself getting distracted from his edits by the thought of pulling her close to tangle his fingers in the silky length.

He couldn't stop looking at her, and she remained

frustratingly unaware. The more things changed, and all that jazz.

The sky was dark behind the windows when Finn finally caught him staring at her. He affected a bored look, hoping it wasn't obvious that he'd been watching her worry her lower lip with her sharp little teeth and imagining it was *his* lip she was nibbling on.

Her eyes widened, her cheeks pinked, and she lurched from her chair. Not so unaware after all, apparently.

"Look at the time!" she blurted, her gaze sliding over his shoulder to the coffee-cup-shaped clock over the sink. "I'm starving. Are you starving?"

Tom blinked slowly, aware she was thinking about a different kind of hunger. "Always. I always want something to eat." He kept his tone light so the double entendre wouldn't be as obvious to her as it was in his suddenly pulsating brain.

"Okay. It won't be fancy," she warned as she turned to rummage through the freezer. "Keep working. It'll be ready in a bit."

Tom wrapped up the last edits on the page as she clattered around with the microwave, and when he joined her at the counter to ask if she needed any help, she waved a plate under his nose. Tom did a double take in astonishment.

"Are those... Oh my God, did you make *chili dogs?*"

She shrugged. "We had some Nathan's Famous in the freezer."

He gripped her upper arms. "You're the perfect woman, and this is the perfect kitchen. I think I live here now."

He could tell the compliment pleased her by the way

she smiled at him without dipping her chin or sliding her eyes away.

"You're ridiculous. Sit down."

She was relaxing in his presence. He saw the starch leaching from her spine. Now to keep the momentum going.

"So, are you an 'all food stays in the kitchen' household?"

"God, no. That couch is mostly made up of Josie's pizza stains." She glanced toward the living room furniture.

"Don't you think it's a shame to let that TV stay unwatched much longer?" he wheedled.

"Well, it *is* Friday night. Couch, TV, and dinner is my traditional 'unplug your brain and celebrate because it's the end of the week' activity."

"Excellent. Wine?"

Another hesitation, and in the end, she shook her head no, so he snagged them each bottles of water from the fridge. She settled on the couch, and he lowered himself into the easy chair he'd occupied the day before, hooking an ankle around the ottoman to bring it close enough to prop his feet on.

She sat with her legs curled underneath her, her plate in her lap, and flipped on the TV.

"What'll it be?" He was curious what TV time looked like for Finn. When he'd known her in high school, she'd worked two after-school jobs and barely had time to sleep, let alone consume pop culture.

She pointed the remote. "Actually, I'm in the middle of watching *Barbarian Time Brigands.*"

After a startled second, he threw his head back in laughter. "You? Little Miss Sci-Fi Is For Dorks?"

"I never said that!" she insisted over his hooting. "Did I?"

He set his plate on the ottoman to wipe his eyes. "Yes! So many times. Do you remember Dylan and me practically bribing you to go see *BTB: Warrior Seasons* with us on opening weekend?"

Her face lit up. "Yes! That's right! You guys bought me Starbucks for a week after that."

"So the great Finn Carey has succumbed to the charms of Griff the time-traveling dragon. What season are you on? Or are you into the movies?"

She navigated through the menu. "I'm in the final season with the original cast, then I'll do the movies, and then I'll start on the reboot. I take it that means you're okay watching it with me?"

"Always. And particularly any season that has Marita Leonard on-screen in body paint."

SEVEN

Finn slept late and woke the next morning to the smell of coffee. After slipping into yoga pants and a fleece, she made a stop in the bathroom to tidy up (including a tiny bit of lip gloss— vanity, thy name is Fiona) and mentally reviewed the options for the day that she'd planned out while trying to fall asleep the night before. But when she padded into the kitchen and found an appealingly sleep-rumpled Tom with stubble darkening his jaw, all other thoughts flew from her head.

"Happy Saturday! I snooped." He held a sheet of paper aloft. "Huckleberry, are you telling me that you inventoried the contents of your pantry and made a list of all the possible meals you could make from those ingredients?"

She yawned and slid into one of the kitchen chairs. "And?"

He ran his eyes down her notes. "And I'm honestly impressed. You could cook a meal for this whole apartment complex or make sure you and I survived in here for three weeks. It's incredibly comprehensive."

She refused to be pleased by his enthusiasm. "I like being prepared."

"Oh, I'm aware." He plunked a mug of coffee in front of her, into which he'd added her preferred splash of cream. "You must've been thrilled when I crashed your blizzard party of one."

She held the mug to her mouth rather than answer. He *had* thrown her for a loop, but now... Well, it wasn't so bad, having him here.

He changed the subject before she succumbed to the temptation to be honest. "So you've got eggs on here. Do you have specific plans for them?"

She had a feeling Tom was about to go off-list with a menu suggestion. In fact, she had a feeling *everything* Tom did was pretty much off-list. "Food plans or life plans?" she hedged. "Because I've been saving up to send those eggs to college. But a state school, not an Ivy."

Tom rolled with the nonsense emerging from her sleep-muddled brain. "Oh, not Yale? In that case, they'd be better off in the omelets I was going to offer to make."

As was becoming common when it came to Tom, she was equal parts horrified and intrigued. He wanted to make a mess in her meticulously organized kitchen? Yet at the same time, there was no sense lying to herself; she really did want to see him make a mess in her meticulously organized kitchen. "You're right. An omelet is the kinder fate. Do you need any help?"

He was already pulling ingredients out of the fridge. "Not if you don't mind my rummaging wantonly through your stuff. I assume you're not morally or allergically opposed to any of the ingredients on your list?"

"Not at all," Finn said after another long slurp of coffee.

"Bacon it is," he said. "Your job is to observe and shout helpful suggestions."

God, it was easy to forget about her anger the longer he was around. And so she let herself, for the moment anyway. She lounged in a chair and pointed out where he could find bowls and pans and knives, teasing him when his diced veggies came out uneven and complimenting him when the beautifully cooked omelet slid right out of the pan in a way hers never did. If having Tom back in her life meant restaurant-quality breakfasts, she could be into that.

"I saw online that the city hopes to start plowing the major thoroughfares this afternoon, and then they'll start working on the smaller streets," he said as he forked a piece of omelet into his mouth.

Ah, of course. He wasn't actually back in her life long-term, and he certainly wouldn't be cooking her breakfast in the future. "Well, this is definitely one of the smaller streets, but I don't think we'll need to ration our food."

"I read your list. We should be fine. I mean, your ice cream stash alone could keep us alive for weeks."

So he'd discovered her vice.

"Apparently heavy snow's snapping power lines all over the city and causing outages," she said. "All I'm saying is this is an old building with old wires, so stashing ice cream in the snow is high on my list of survival plans."

"Speaking of plans," he said. "It sounds like we have to coexist for another day at least. So I figure we've got two options."

"Two options," she parroted, choking back a laugh that she'd come to the kitchen armed with plans for the day, but roll-with-the-punches-Tom had beaten her to it.

"Yes, two options," he said. "One, I still have a mountain of editing, so like we've been doing, we can work until it's time for dinner, TV, and bed. Or two: We declare today a lazy day and lounge."

His fork clinked against his plate as he waited for her response.

"Funny," she said. "I came up with three options as I was falling asleep last night." He didn't need to know she'd written them down and numbered them in order of preference in the Bullet Journal she kept on her nightstand.

"Excellent. Hit me."

"Well, there's plan A: we can keep plugging away on our projects. Plan B: we can fire up Netflix. Or plan C: we can spend all day in bed, reading and napping."

He quirked a brow at her. "In bed? Sounds heavenly."

The words scorched the air around her. She hadn't meant to say that, but it slipped out and now the image throbbed in her brain. Tom, sprawled across her bed, curly head propped on his hand while the other held a book. Setting it aside when he noticed her eyes drifting shut and then wrapping them both in a blanket. Napping together and waking to find his hand sliding under her clothes, seeking—

Her cheeks heated, and she reached for her coffee mug to halt her wayward thoughts. *That* wasn't part of the plan.

"Different beds and different bedrooms of course," she clarified, inwardly wincing at her prissy tone. "Speaking of, have you gotten over feeling weird about being in Josie's room?"

He shrugged. "I still wake up feeling like a stranger in a strange land."

She didn't buy that for a second.

"But you're *you*. You're not a stranger anywhere you go."

He looked up from his plate and waved his fork in a circle. "Explain."

Oh Lord. She'd said too much, but now he was looking at her with curious eyes, so she babbled on. "Well, look at you. You're cooking in my kitchen. You've kept a conversation going with me like no time's passed at all. You're acting like you can just forget that thing our senior year ever happened. You're unstoppable."

He chewed a bite of omelet and swallowed, then wiped his mouth on a napkin. "I'm an extrovert. Guilty. When I'm an old man, I'll be that person talking to himself on the L platform because I love the sound of my own voice. But as for that thing in high school, I did try to bring it up the first night, and you didn't want to talk about it, so hell, why *not* pretend it never happened?"

She scoffed, then filled her mouth with omelet to keep from saying anything else stupid.

He lowered his fork. "What?"

She took her time chewing and swallowing. "Easy for you to say."

He suddenly looked a lot less relaxed. "Excuse me?"

She regretted bringing it up but forged ahead anyway. "I mean, *I* was the one who got humiliated. It just made *you* look like a jerk."

Tom made an elaborate show of looking over his left shoulder, then his right one. "Weird. I don't *see* the asshole responsible sitting at this table."

She slammed her coffee cup down as the memory of Tom's old betrayal resurfaced to hook its claws into her brain. "You're joking, right? You shared a text I sent you, a *private* text, with the whole school. You called me a *slut*. Textbook asshole as far as I'm concerned."

Although his hands balled into fists on the tabletop, he spoke in a flat voice. "I was a dumb kid in high school, but I thought you knew me better than that."

"I texted you that I wanted to end things with Dylan. I said..."

She swallowed convulsively, amazed at the capacity of that old hurt to conjure fresh pain. *I'm going to break up with Dylan. I need to be with someone who really sees me.* She'd texted that to Tom between math class and PE the last week of their senior year. And she'd waited for his reply with her heart lodged in her throat, praying he'd understand what she was asking: *Do you see me the way I think you do? Should I really be with you instead?* But by the time she'd changed into her gym clothes and made it outside, she was greeted with a hissed chorus of "whore" and "I'll give you that D" from the smirking classmates lying in wait for her on the rubber track.

"You put the screenshot in the class Facebook group." She closed her eyes as she recited the words, unable to look at the grim face of the man across from her. "'The quarterback's slut wants to get laid. Who's got next?'" Words she'd never been able to shake. Words that still hit like a punch to the gut.

"How can you still think it was me?"

Her eyes flew open at the harsh rasp in Tom's voice. "Because I sent it to *you*, and then it ended up online!"

He banged a fist on the table, sending a spoon clattering to the floor. "Oh, and our phones were so secure back then, right? It's not like it took a team of hackers weeks and weeks to crack my shit. It probably took Dylan all of thirty seconds to post that from my phone."

"Sure, Dylan just happened to be holding your phone when I texted you my secret desire to break up with him." She scoffed, but she struggled to put any heat behind it. Was he really trying to tell her it hadn't been him?

"The Castle bad luck." Tom grimaced and plunged a hand through his already disheveled curls. "He was borrowing mine for the calculator because his battery was dead."

She opened her mouth, then closed it again as her mind worked. She'd spent years wondering how the Tom she'd known could be capable of something so ugly, and she'd never truly been able to reconcile his actions with the person who'd been her closest friend. Still, one detail stuck in her mind from that horrible afternoon, and it's what had convinced her that she didn't know Tom at all.

"You laughed," she said quietly.

"I *what?*" He flung his arms out.

"You heard me." *Now* she found the fire to put behind her words. "You laughed when I finally found you."

His cheeks flushed as his voice grew louder. "You came running to me in your gym clothes in tears. I thought you were in pain. I thought somebody *hurt* you."

She surged to her feet. "*You* hurt me! And then you laughed!"

He stood too. "Because I was so relieved that you weren't bleeding from a stab wound or something!" Her mouth worked, but no sound came out so he kept talking. "But you ran off before I could figure out what was going on, and once I did, I got to a computer lab and deleted it. But then you never spoke to me again. You avoided me, presumably blocked my number. You never let me explain."

She clenched her teeth at his injured tone. Was he

seriously trying to make himself the victim? "Of course I avoided you! My text was posted from your account. What was I supposed think?"

His glittering eyes bored into hers. "You were supposed to know me better than anybody else in my life. You should've trusted that I would never do that to you when all I ever wanted was—"

He blinked rapidly, choking on the words, and silence stretched between them until Finn spat out, "Fucking Dylan."

"Fucking Dylan." Tom forcefully agreed. "I take it he never had the balls to tell you he was behind it all?"

She shook her head, her brain churning as she processed this new information. Of *course* Dylan. His selfishness had bothered her from time to time when they were together, and then she'd become horribly aware of his cruelty after they'd split up and he'd mounted a campaign to ostracize her during the last week of high school. But even then, all she'd been able to see were Tom's face and name next to that vile post that haunted her. The betrayal she never saw coming. The cruelty that had hurt the most.

But it was Dylan, not Tom, this whole time. She pressed a hand to her churning stomach as she struggled to make sense of the new villain in her life.

"And?" Tom asked.

She shook her head in confusion, so he clarified. "Dylan. Are you still pissed at him?"

The sharp question threw her. "I broke up with him, didn't I?"

"Sure, eight years ago, but are you pissed at him *right now*?" He stepped closer, so close she could smell the soap from her shower on his skin. It made her head spin, and she spoke in a rush.

"Honestly, I don't give a shit about Dylan."

His voice dropped. "Then I don't understand why you're still pissed at *me*."

She wanted to tell him that was ridiculous, that she'd gotten over her anger ages ago, because holding on to it for all this time was unreasonable. Yet when she opened her mouth, the truth spilled out. "I *am* still pissed. You were the best guy I knew."

His mouth flattened. "But he was the one you were dating."

"Well, you were dating *every girl in our class!*"

"Only because the girl I *wanted* was dating my best friend!"

They were standing toe to toe now, yelling again, and for a moment the only sound was the rasping of their breath as the realization of what Tom had said coursed through her body like fast-moving lava. Her skin heated, and the blood pounded so hard in her temples that the air around them flickered and her eyesight started to fade.

Wait, that wasn't her eyes. That was the electric grid. They both glanced up as the overhead lights blinked off, then back on for a millisecond before flickering off again, plunging the room into darkness.

EIGHT

Tom's heart thundered in the sudden blackness.

Fuck. He hadn't meant to shout his deepest secrets at her, and he'd seen understanding click in her brain right before the lights blinked out. He might as well have fallen to his knees and announced how much he used to love her.

Next to him in the dark, Finn exhaled slowly. "Tom, I... I didn't... I never..."

Her voice sounded small after the volume of their fight, and his heart plummeted every time she started a sentence but didn't finish it.

"You seriously had no idea how I felt?" He matched her hushed tones, the darkness making the question easier to ask. He couldn't see her, so he wouldn't be distracted by her big brown eyes. Wouldn't have to watch her let him down easy.

The air next to him stirred. "I wasn't sure. I sometimes wondered if..." She sighed. "I guess it stopped mattering after all that."

It hadn't stopped mattering to *him*, and he cleared his

throat against the tightness lingering there to say something he should've said years ago. "I'm so sorry, Finn." Exposing this particular vein was painful, even all these years later, but he'd do it. He'd drag his blood and his guts to the surface if she asked him to. "I was so pissed at you for thinking I was capable of doing that. By the time I cooled down and realized how it looked, that you deserved an explanation about what actually happened, we weren't..."

She picked up his unfinished thought, her voice sounding mournful in the dark. "We weren't friends anymore."

Friends. The word sat on his tongue, filling his mouth with a familiar bitterness. Yet hadn't she just implied that she was put out by his dating other girls in high school? Was it possible she'd felt something for him too?

"I missed you, Tom."

Her confession startled him, and *now* he wanted the light. He wanted to study her face, to see if she missed her friend Tom, or if she missed him for bigger reasons than that. But the power stayed stubbornly off, and her whispered words didn't reveal what was in her heart. Still, she'd said "friends," so Tom squeezed his eyes shut in the middle of the darkness and reminded himself of how well he played the look-what-great-buds-we-are game. He could do that again if that's what she needed.

"I missed you too. What's Tom Sawyer without Huckleberry Finn?" Their old joke earned him a watery laugh in the darkness, and it was enough to get him moving onto a less dangerous topic. "Okay, let's get some light in here. Do you have candles or anything?"

"Oh! I've got something better."

Her voice was back to its normal volume, and as she

moved away from him, he navigated toward the windows and pulled back the curtains, allowing thin gray light from the overcast sky to trickle in. "Looks like the power's out for the whole street."

"It happened once before during a big storm," she called from the hallway. "Then it was fixed in a few hours, but who knows with all this snow."

The ambient light was enough for him to see her outline plunk something down on the coffee table in the living room. Then with a "voilà!" she switched on a camping lantern that emitted a welcoming yellow glow in a ten-foot circumference. "Battery operated LEDs. It'll last up to a week, allegedly."

When he shot her a questioning look, she shrugged. "That guy whose clothes you're wearing? Richard? He likes camping, so Josie and I have some weird outdoors equipment we've picked up over the years."

Boy howdy did Tom have questions about Richard the camping god, but he bit them back and took a seat in his favorite chair. Finn chose her usual spot on the far edge of the couch, where the warm light glinted off her hair. Now that their storm of angry words had ended, he wasn't sure where that left them.

"So, uh, how's Dylan these days?" she asked casually.

Christ, he never wanted to hear that guy's name again. "No idea."

"Really? I assumed you two—"

"The last time he and I spoke, I punched him in the face. That pretty well ended the friendship."

Finn's mouth dropped. "Is *that* why he had a black eye at graduation?" At Tom's nod, she jutted her chin. "Good. After what he did, he didn't deserve either of us."

"Yeah, by then he was a completely different guy than

the one I met in kindergarten." He answered on automatic while his brain worked overtime to process her words.

She believed him. Like a footprint in the sand that slowly filled with water, the realization trickled into the hollow in his heart that her mistrust had created. And like that, he was tempted to throw himself at her feet. Instead, he borrowed her tactic. "And what about you? How bad was it for you after that?"

Finn's smile didn't quite reach her eyes. "It wasn't great. But we only had one week of school left, so I kind of acted like a ghost. And enough people knew what kind of guy Dylan was that a few were sympathetic. Still, I was glad for a fresh start at college. I considered myself reborn at UIC."

"And were you? Reborn?"

She exhaled a laugh. "Yes. College was great. I rose from the ashes of high school like a very popular phoenix. I met Josie, joined a sorority, dated some nice boys. It was good to find out that I wasn't permanently damaged."

He studied his feet propped on the ottoman, this time covered in fuzzy polka dots from Finn's warm sock collection. "I try to do right by women now."

His non sequitur surprised him, and it confused Finn even more. "What do you mean?"

He hesitated, not particularly enjoying analyzing how his teenage mistakes had turned him into the person he was today. "It's about more than just not being an asshole toward women. It's about standing up to guys who are." He shrugged. "I didn't do a good job back then, and I made more excuses than I should have for someone I thought was a friend. Since then, I've tried to be better."

She made a soft, understanding noise. "Like making

sure my roommate got home safely when she had too much to drink, even though you were dead on your feet from exhaustion and malnutrition?" It wasn't so dim that he couldn't see her small smile.

"Something like that." He kept his tone light, but in truth, he wanted to bask in her approval and wrap it around him like a cape. The thrill her smile created settled briefly in his heart before traveling straight to his groin.

He cleared his throat and said briskly, "So it's option three then."

She looked at him blankly.

"Our plans for the rest of our day?" he reminded her. "We've got no TV, no Wi-Fi. We should probably conserve our laptop batteries. That knocks out your first and second options and leaves us with option three."

"Right. We go to our rooms to read."

Rooms, plural. Had one little *s* ever caused such plunging disappointment before? He was preparing to engage friend-mode Tom and exile himself to Josie's pink bedroom when Finn spoke again.

"Oh, but actually..."

Tom held his breath, daring to unfurl a tendril of hope.

"I mean, we only have one lantern, so separate rooms wouldn't work," she said. "Want to stay out here?"

Separate rooms were definitely safer for his wayward thoughts. But what's life without a little danger? "Sounds perfect."

He fetched his e-reader from his bag while Finn retrieved a book from her room.

Back in their positions, he pointed to the massive tome on her lap. "That's a doorstop."

"I'm *yet again* trying to get through *Infinite Jest*. Someday I need to admit to myself that I wasn't built to read this book. What about you?"

He powered on his Kindle, grateful to see a full battery icon. "While I'm doing dissertation edits, I limit myself to comfort reading. I just started one of my favorite Terry Pratchett books."

She brightened. "I've heard he's funny!"

"He's hilarious. Actually..." Was he really going to suggest this? "If you're not into your David Foster Wallace, I could, um, read *The Color of Magic* to you."

He was excruciatingly aware of every moment of silence that stretched between them after his impulsive suggestion, unsure if he'd had a good idea or the worst one ever. Then, thank the giant space turtle, she grinned up at him. "Will you do voices? And accents?"

He'd definitely had a good idea. "Voices, yes. Accents, badly."

"Awesome. Let's do it."

Finn repositioned herself on the end of the couch nearest to him, an afghan tucked around her shoulders and a half smile on her lips, and he pushed aside his unaccustomed bout of nerves to get comfortable in his chair and began narrating the story of the wizard Rincewind from page one.

He read to her for hours. His voice grew hoarse as he deepened it for the barbarian and squeaked for the sea troll, but he read on and on. They took a break for sandwiches and wine, and when they returned to the living room, Tom made the bold move of sitting with her on the couch. Not only did Finn not object, but she stretched out, her legs draped over the sofa arm and the top of her head brushing his thigh.

Now the hoarseness in his voice could be attributed to a different source, and he gingerly slid a hand along her silky hair. When she didn't move away, he caressed the strands to the rhythm of the dialogue as he read. Eventually her breathing evened and slowed so much that he wondered if she'd fallen asleep. He stopped his narration, and after a moment, she stirred, twisting her neck to look up at him.

His hand stilled. "Are you tired of the story?"

"No."

"Should I keep going?" He couldn't read what was happening behind her serious eyes.

"I just... I keep thinking about what you said earlier."

His shoulders tensed. "Yes?" He'd said a lot of things earlier.

"I met him first."

"Sorry?" His breath caught in his throat as she rolled to her back and looked up at him.

"Dylan. I met him first. He was so handsome, and he was a football star. I thought he was what I wanted. He was what all the other girls wanted. But then he introduced me to you."

Tom's lungs stopped working entirely, along with his heart and his ability to speak.

"You were so different from him." Finn sighed.

"Yeah." He offered a self-deprecating laugh, while inside part of him withered. "Not handsome. And not a football star."

"Thank God for that last one. And you were totally handsome, you goof." Her quicksilver smile appeared and vanished again just as quickly. "At first I was glad my boyfriend's best friend liked me. And then I started spending more time with you, and you actually listened to me when I talked, way better than he did. You came to my show choir concerts. You sat with me in the ER when my brother broke his arm..."

He tipped his head back and stared at the ceiling, awash in the memory of the love and the helpless longing he used to feel for her. With effort, he wrestled those old emotions under control. "It's an old story. They write songs about it: 'my best friend's girl' and all that." He forced himself to sound flippant and indulged in another slide of his fingers along her scalp. "I tried like hell not to let you know how I felt back then."

"I couldn't imagine you'd be interested in me like that. I just thought you liked spending time with me even when Dylan was off doing two-a-days or whatever."

"I *did* like spending time with you."

"But you were so busy with other girls," she said, closing her eyes.

He gave a rueful laugh. "They were supposed to keep my mind off you, not that it worked. None of them measured up."

Her eyes fluttered open to stare at the ceiling, but she said nothing. Meanwhile, his mind churned. What if he hadn't dated around? What if he'd been honest with her? Would she actually have broken up with Dylan to be with him? It was impossible to know, so he kept stroking her hair and imagined a world where this was how they'd spent every Saturday for the past decade.

The soft lighting and the heat of her body next to him made honesty easy. "I grew out of dating everything that moves a long time ago, just so you know."

"Oh, so you're a monk now?"

Her voice wasn't accusatory, but he offered a mild

defense anyway. "I'm far more monkish than anything else these days."

Wow, Castle, way to impress her with your prowess. But what was the point of pretending? He still hadn't found anyone who made him feel like Finn had.

She interrupted his wayward thoughts by tipping her head back to smile up at him. "Okay, mister monk. The power doesn't seem to magically be coming back on, and you left off on a cliffhanger. Better start the next chapter."

NINE

Finn's leg was asleep, she was freezing, and her left sock had twisted around until the heel was on top of her foot, but none of that mattered. She didn't want to move from this spot, ever, because Tom Castle was running his fingers through her hair and reading out loud to her in a charmingly earnest manner that filled her with such joy she didn't know how flowers weren't bursting into bloom on her skin.

"Is this a good stopping point?" Tom asked. He set his e-reader down but didn't still the movements of his fingers.

"No. Never stop." The words came out closer to a moan, and to her chagrin, he *did* stop playing with her hair. Wondering why she sounded like a wounded animal probably.

As her senses slowly returned, she became aware of the temperature in the apartment. She sat up regretfully and pulled the afghan more tightly around her. "I didn't realize how cold it got in here."

"No power, no heat. The temperature's been dropping all afternoon." He gave a little shiver.

"You may freeze to death yet. I pulled you off the streets for nothing."

"Not for nothing. I made you an omelet." He yawned and stretched. "Please tell me this mysterious 'Richard' left behind some fleece-lined sweatshirts or long johns or something."

She shook her head. "I don't think so. I'll have to check, but it's probably all workout gear. And what's with the air quotes?"

He shot her an innocent look. "What, you mean 'Richard'?" He busted out the air quotes again. "I mean, he *is* real, right? You don't actually keep clothes on hand to dress your male guests like a Ken doll?"

Ha. Their last male guest had been... well, Richard.

"What could you possibly know about Ken?" she teased.

"I know he's unfortunately smooth in important places." Tom flashed his dimples, which naturally made her think about his nonsmooth places and—

Nope. No more lecherous thoughts for the night.

"I'll have you know that Richard is very real," she said primly, bending down to adjust her damn sock.

Tom opened his mouth, then shut it, then opened it again. "I mean, is 'Richard'"—air quotes again—"a boyfriend? Your personal trainer? Your bodyguard? Not that it's my business. It's just, I *am* wearing his clothes." He traced his finger around the rim of his wineglass, the corners of his mouth twisting downward. Was he asking because he was curious? Could he be... was he maybe... *jealous?*

Finn snatched the opportunity to stretch this out a bit

and see what would happen. "Oh, Richard's great. I met him through Josie. He works for one of the big event-planning companies in town, which means he always gets me into the coolest fund-raisers and galas as his date. Although we always have to wear the big credential lanyards, which totally spoil the lines of my gowns."

Tom grimaced. "Okay, so Richard's tall and in decent shape, I assume, since I can wear his clothes. And he likes camping, which probably makes him a guy's guy. And he takes the ladies to all the nice events in the city, so he's an in-demand date. I... I think I might hate him a little," he concluded glumly.

Finn bit her lip to keep from smiling. "Oh, he's a very in-demand date. And he loves going with me to the charity galas because they're such great places to meet guys." She watched Tom closely in the light of the lantern and saw one corner of his mouth hitch upward as he processed what she'd said.

Those dimples. Those dimples were going to kill her.

He relaxed back into the couch, stretching his arm along the back. "Great places to meet guys, huh? So who has better luck at these fund-raisers, him or you?" His amber eyes were warm on hers as he waited for an answer.

"Him, definitely. I'm bad at chatting up men."

"I would disagree."

All possible responses fled amid a storm of flutters in her stomach. Luckily, she was saved from responding when her phone chirped with a text. She leaned forward to pluck it off the table.

Josie: *Still alive?*
Finn: *Barely. We lost power.*
Josie: *Yikes. You doing okay?*

Finn didn't even hesitate. *All good! Thank God for Richard's lantern.*

Josie: *Richard thanks God for his lantern every night, if u know what I mean. Hey, did u see a note for me lying around anywhere on Thursday?*

Now she hesitated. Josie had to be referring to a possible note from Tom, but Finn didn't relish explaining the current situation over text. So she kicked the can down the road for Future Finn to deal with at a later date when Tom wasn't quite so... present and touchable on her couch.

Finn: *Nope, no note.*

Technically true.

Josie: *Dammit. Okay, I'm off to prowl the strip. Return flight Monday night. XO*

Well, look at that. Finn had escaped without mentioning her houseguest. Josie was due back two days from now, which gave the city plenty of time to clear the streets and sidewalks. Tom would leave and go back to being part of Finn's past, and she'd never have to explain that she'd spent a few strange days repairing old hurts with the man who'd walked Josie home on Wednesday night. Unless...

What if Tom decided he didn't want to be a monk anymore? He could easily take the note with Josie's phone number and call her sometime. What if he came by the apartment to pick her up for a date? Oh God, what if he stayed overnight for nonchivalrous reasons and Finn bumped into him in the morning over coffee?

This is where her plan-happy brain was a curse. She leaped ahead to future possibilities, and in this case, they weren't pretty. Imagining Tom and Josie together...

"Hey, everything okay over there?"

Tom's words interrupted her runaway worst-case-scenario musings, and she forced a smile.

"Yep. My mom asking how the storm is." That was also technically true, as she had a dozen concerned-mom texts on her phone, requesting a status report. She swiftly tapped out "All good here! Snug inside!" and hit Send. After all, she didn't *need* to remind Tom about her vivacious, attractive roommate, right?

With that thought, a yawn overtook her, likely the result of an overly emotional day. "I should head to bed."

"Me too," he said. "What do you think about my chopping up your coffee table for kindling? We could make a fire in the bathtub to keep us warm."

Finn hopped to her feet. "Pretty sure Richard doesn't have an ax in his supply stash."

"That's a shame. As a dude, I'm not allowed to admit that extreme temperatures bother me, but damn, it's getting cold in here." He shivered again, then shot her a sheepish smile, and her brain shouted, *Body heat! Body heat will keep us warm!*

Once the thought popped into her head, she struggled to think of anything—*anything*—other than her big bed. *Tom* in her big bed. But of course that wasn't on the menu. He had a bed he was sleeping in, so she'd go to her corner and he to his. Still, no reason for them to unnecessarily suffer. She shuffled to the linen closet and pulled out the extra blankets they kept in the house. It was a pitifully small pile, and Tom selected the thinnest one.

"It's fine," he said when she protested. "Can't have the delicate lady catching a chill."

"How positively Victorian of you. Do you swear you're not planning to sacrifice your toes to frostbite out of misplaced nobility?"

"Absolutely not. I'm fond of my toes, and they're currently covered by your ridiculous fuzzy socks. I'm not worried."

With that settled, they took turns in the bathroom, then Finn retreated to her room and did her best to make a nest of the blankets to trap whatever warmth she could. The snow might have stopped coming down, but subzero temperatures had taken over during this wretched weather weekend, and even bundled up she felt the chill creeping through the single-pane window in her bedroom to wrap its tentacles around her limbs.

She fell into an uneasy sleep that only lasted a few hours. When she woke up, the tip of her nose was cold to the touch, and she was shivering under the layers of blankets.

Another pair of socks. Another sweatshirt. Maybe even her cable-knit hat. If she could will herself out of her cocoon, she could arm herself with another layer of clothing. She braced herself, shrugged off the blankets, and exposed her body to the cold air, wincing as she pulled on more socks. Then she rushed down the hall toward the coatrack next to the front door where she rooted through the basket of outerwear until she found her hat.

When Josie's bedroom door creaked open, she froze. Tom, silhouetted in the gloom, stood in the doorway with a blanket wrapped around him like a cape.

"I may have underestimated the odds of frostbite," he said with a chattering of his teeth. "I think it's time we come up with another plan."

TEN

Tom knew what he had to suggest. It was the only thing that made sense. And he was far, far too excited about it, which meant he needed to find a way to make the suggestion without sounding like the creep Finn had thought he was until about twelve hours ago.

"So I've—" he began, but she cut him off.

"Will you sleep with me?"

The blanket slipped from his numb fingers to puddle at his feet as Finn made a strangled sound.

"I mean, *oh my God,* not *that.* But I think maybe if we shared blankets, we might be warmer. In the same bed. Wearing clothes."

Even though sharing a bed and blankets and body heat had been the same thing he was thinking, her words still left him momentarily mute.

"Never mind. I'm walking outside now," she muttered. "Let the blizzard claim me."

"No!" He lurched forward. "I was going to suggest the same thing. It's the smartest option." Smart. Yep, this was purely a matter of survival. "So, uh, your room or mine-slash-your roommate's?"

"Mine of course. Do you want me to dig up a hat or gloves for you from the stash?"

It was a good idea, but no way was Tom covering his hands if they'd be anywhere near Finn's skin. "Nah, I'll give it a go without."

He crossed to the threshold of her room and paused. The memory of Finn's head resting on his leg while he'd read to her on the couch had kept him up—yes, *literally* up—and now he was about to crawl under the covers with her.

You can do this. Don't make this weird. She's only being practical, and so are you.

"Which side?" His voice rasped, and he prayed she'd chalk it up to the late hour and the amount of reading aloud earlier.

When she pointed to the right, he went obediently, dragging the blankets he'd stolen from Josie's bed. Finn slid into the other side, and together they layered the blankets around and on top of themselves. When they were done, they were tucked in and bundled so tightly that he could barely move, with Finn as a little mound of fabric next to him.

"Better?" he murmured.

"Yes," she said with a sigh.

A shiver ran through her body, and he edged closer to her, wanting to shield her from the temperature.

"I used a little battery to check the news on my phone." He spoke into the dark, not ready to fall asleep quite yet. "Sounds like the power company's working overtime to get everything restored."

"I don't envy them." She shuddered, which shifted her close enough that her hat brushed the tip of his nose.

"The offer still stands to chop your furniture into a burn pile."

Her elbow connected with his midsection, although the impact was blunted by the three shirts he was wearing.

They lapsed into silence, but the cadence of her breathing suggested that she wasn't close to sleep yet.

"Tom?"

"Hmm?"

She rolled to face him, and the moon offered enough light for him to see the silvery outline of her features. "Just curious. How many of your students are in love with you?"

He huffed a laugh at the unexpected question. "*That's* what you want to know? All the ground we've covered today, the deep dark secrets we've revealed, the new depths we've explored, and you want to know how many eighteen-year-olds hang around after my lectures to ask if I have a girlfriend?"

"Yes. Obviously."

He rolled so they were face-to-face. "I'm a twenty-six-year-old authority figure to them. You wouldn't think very highly of me if I kept track. *I* wouldn't think very highly of me if I kept track."

She smirked. "I'm taking that to mean 'All of them. All my students are in love with me.'"

He shrugged, uneasy with the whole topic. "Who knew economics was so sexy? I always politely ignore them and keep grading their papers."

She heaved a sigh. "Those poor kids. I don't know

what I would've done if my TAs had been half as hot as you."

Finn thought he was hot. Finn. Thought he. Was hot. The realization sped from his brain to points south, and he shifted fractionally to keep those southern points away from the woman lying next to him.

"What do you want to do after you finish your dissertation?" she asked.

Yeah, that killed the vibe. With a groan, he rolled onto his back and stared holes into the ceiling. Looked like uncertainty about the future could keep him awake in places other than his tiny grad-student apartment.

"Mostly I want to finish. I'm in the final stages, but it still feels like I have to scale a whole mountain range with a bag of rocks on my back. After that, I dunno... become a professor? Work for a think tank or a hedge fund? Revolutionize the field with my new theories on the hidden benefits of ethical investing?"

Ridiculous to feel paralyzed by options, yet here he was. Then Finn chased away his apprehensions by saying, "New plan: You save the world as a masked superhero economics guy."

He ran with it, happy for now to choose levity over concerns about his future. "Captain Capitalism. Less swole than Captain America, but with a better stock portfolio."

She rewarded his dad joke with a giggle. A shame though, for her to laugh in the dark. It meant he wasn't able to enjoy the shape of her lips as they curved upward and begged to be kissed.

"How about you? Is marketing your forever calling?"

She burrowed closer to him. She actually *burrowed*. The room was frigid, but Tom was starting to sweat.

"Yes, actually. I love it. Someday I'd like to open my own agency, be the boss, choose my own clients."

"I think that makes *you* Captain Capitalism."

"I bet my costume's cuter than yours."

"I bet it is."

Their words drifted away, and Tom breathed in the scent of her on the pillowcase and enjoyed the silence that enveloped them. Finn must have had a similar thought because she said sleepily, "The street's usually so much noisier. This is nice."

Another wriggle moved her even closer until her head rested against his shoulder. He slid an arm under her, prepared to yank it back if she objected.

She didn't, so he tightened his hold. "Are you warmer now?"

He took her contented little noise to mean yes, so he closed his eyes and willed his body to relax and his brain to shut off while her cold nose pressed against his jaw.

"Tom?"

She sounded so adorably drowsy that he couldn't help pressing his lips to the top of her head, even though she likely couldn't feel it through her hat. "Yes, Huck?"

"I'm glad you passed out after walking Josie home."

His heart squeezed.

"Even though my being here likely cursed the power lines?"

Her breath tickled his neck as she sighed. "I'm glad about that too."

ELEVEN

For the second day in a row, Finn awoke to the smell of coffee.

Her sleepy brain caught up slowly.

Coffee meant electricity. Electricity meant heat. Heat meant she didn't need to cling to Tom like a limpet in order to survive the harsh terrain of her apartment. Back to separate couches and separate beds.

The thought was surprisingly disappointing.

She struggled to sit up amid the nest they'd made and pulled off the outer layers of her cold-weather gear, immediately feeling less like the kid brother in *A Christmas Story*. The tip of her nose was no longer numb, and her phone case was no longer cold to the touch.

She was about to force herself out of bed when Tom entered, carrying two mugs.

"Good morning. I bring caffeine."

He too had shed a few of his layers, giving her a pleasing eyeful of his strong, lean body under Richard's almost-the-right-size clothes. He handed her a mug, and she slurped down half the hot beverage with one long swallow.

"This is the best coffee I've ever had. I could kiss you."

It took a moment for her brain, still a wee bit sluggish, to process what she'd said.

Not Tom though. Without a word, he took the half-empty coffee cup from her and placed it next to his on the bedside table. Then he turned back to her and put both hands on her jaw, running his thumbs lightly over the crest of her cheekbones.

"Okay."

"Okay?" she whispered as her heartbeat kicked into overdrive.

"Okay," he repeated. "You should kiss me."

So she did. She stopped thinking ahead, stopped trying to plan, stopped worrying about the *what ifs* and the *maybe nots*. She leaned forward and pressed her lips against his, gently at first and then with more force. He slid a hand into her sleep-tangled hair, and she opened her mouth to his, tasting the coffee on his tongue and wanting more.

She grabbed the front of his T-shirt and pulled him forward. He complied, leaning to settle one knee on the bed next to her. His lips sliding over hers left sparks in their wake, and how had she ever thought that this man would ever betray her trust? She pulled back to look at him, and his amber eyes glowed with need, delight, vulnerability.

"More," she demanded, and now he was lying next to her, wrapping his arm around her waist to pull her toward him, never breaking their kiss. Then she was the one touching his hair, marveling at the soft curls. Kissing Tom felt *right*, like a homecoming she hadn't known she was missing. But it still wasn't enough.

"More," she panted, and he shifted his body on top of hers, settling his thigh between her legs. She felt him hard against her hip, and she rocked against him, breathing a shaky sigh into his mouth as she started to move in a rhythm that caused her to see stars and him to tighten his grip.

"*More.*" Tom was the one rasping the command now, and she complied, twining her leg around his and pressing herself harder against that long length that she wanted inside her. Her bedroom wasn't cold any longer. She couldn't remember a time when she'd *ever* been cold in fact. Not when her whole body felt like it was on fire. Not when Tom's hand worked its way under the layers of clothing and drifted up... up... up...

Her phone went off.

At first she tried to ignore it, but it kept ringing. The longer it rang, the slower Tom's kissing became, and suddenly his hand was no longer exploring the sensitive skin under her breast.

"Finn. You should answer." The words brushed across the skin behind her ear, which he was exploring with his lips.

"Don't want to," she grumbled, seeking his mouth again.

"Whoever it is sounds like they're going to keep calling."

At Tom's words, the chiming sound clicked in her brain.

"Oh God. It's my brother. I'm always the one who calls him, so I forgot what his ringtone sounds like."

They both scrambled to sit up, and she grabbed her phone. "Hey, jerk."

"Jerk? *I'm* the jerk?" Jake's voice thundered down the line, a mixture of relief and irritation. "I just read your text about letting some guy stay with you this weekend, and then you don't pick up the first two times I call?"

She rolled her eyes. "Oh my God, I'm fine."

Well, she wasn't fine about being interrupted mid make out, and she was guessing Tom wasn't either, judging by the whiteness of his knuckles where he gripped the blankets at the end of the bed.

"You're lucky I didn't call Mom."

"You wouldn't!" Finn leaped off the bed at that thought. "Jake, swear you won't tell Mom. I haven't mentioned that anybody's staying with me when we've texted."

"I really should." Jake sighed. "I mean, Tom? The guy who posted your texts in high school?"

Finn held her breath, hoping that Tom hadn't heard Jake's words. His face was neutral as he stood, grabbed his coffee, and left the room. Once he was gone, she returned her attention to her brother.

"Turns out, I misjudged him. Badly," she said quietly. How bizarre, to have become Tom's defender. "It was a weird coincidence that got us stuck together this weekend, that's all." Then a thought hit her. "Wait, why are you concerned *now*? I texted you Thursday night!"

Jake's voice turned sheepish. "I, ah, didn't see it until five minutes ago."

"It's Sunday, Jake!" Now it was Finn's turn to sigh. "Let me guess. You've used this blizzard weekend to work nonstop, and you haven't taken the time to check your phone."

"Um" was all he offered in his own defense.

Finn had learned one thing growing up with a driven, perfectionist brother who'd worked every day of his life to lift their little family out of dire economic straits: the best defense was a good offense. Jake's lack of a social life was the one thing he didn't want to admit was less than satisfactory, and bringing it up was a low blow. But she had to do something to cut off the lecture about personal responsibility and good choices that she sensed brewing.

"You are aware it's the weekend, right? And that normal people go home at five on Friday and then spend the next two days having fun with their friends? A girlfriend even?"

"I'm not having this discussion again." His voice took on the brother-knows-best tone she hated. "You know I'm on the partnership track, and that's what matters."

"But is it wise to put everything on hold while you chase that sweet, sweet corner office?"

Sadly, Jake and his one-track mind couldn't be distracted. "Let me talk to the guy."

"Absolutely not." Finn wouldn't be budging on that.

"Fine," he snapped after a brief silence-off, sounding exactly like the bossy sixteen-year-old he used to be. It made her smile. Workaholic or not, she missed him.

"At least promise me that you didn't spend this weekend literally snowed in *at the office*."

"Hey, would you look at the time? I really need to go."

Oh, *now* he wanted to get off the phone. She'd bet everything in her bank account that he was sleeping on his office couch so he wouldn't miss any useful working hours.

"Let's get lunch once the snow clears up," she

suggested. Her brother would make time for her. Probably.

"Maybe in a few weeks," he said vaguely, promising nothing. "And tell Tom that if he makes you cry again, I'll break his fucking face."

He hung up before she could respond, and she tossed the phone down on her bed with a growl. She loved her stupid brother, but his timing really sucked.

She grabbed her coffee off the bedside table and took a sip, discovering it was cooling as quickly as the feeling of Tom's lips on hers. Man. What a waste of momentum.

And now she had to walk out of her bedroom and face him. What could she possibly say? No way did she have the courage to ask him to start up where they left off. Did she?

In the kitchen, she found him at the table, working at his computer.

"Yay for power," he said drily. "I can get on with my edits."

Finn blinked. He'd transitioned from starring in the hottest make out session of her life to fiddling with macroeconomic theories? That wasn't good. Apparently the experience didn't rate the same for him.

"Everything okay with your brother?"

"Yeah, he—"

But she was interrupted by a terrible sound. The most unwelcome sound in the world.

A snowplow.

TWELVE

Tom felt the noise of the plow on the asphalt like a physical scrape along his skin.

The plow meant freedom. Freedom meant an end to the strangest and best few days of his life.

He wasn't ready for this to be over.

He stood and walked to the windows where the view confirmed his fears: the big blade of the plow was creating an ever-expanding path that would lead him to public transportation and back to his regularly scheduled life.

"Looks like you're about to have your apartment to yourself," he said when Finn joined him. "Better late than never, right?"

"Right," she replied, staring at the street with a crease in her brow.

And honestly, it was time. He hadn't intentionally listened to her conversation with her brother, but he'd picked up enough words before he slid out of the room to know that even though Jake was five years older than him and Finn, her protective older brother was familiar with the rough outline of the slut-shaming Facebook saga. Jake had it as wrong as everybody else, but his disapproval wasn't a vote in favor of Tom hanging around for any longer than necessary.

Farther down the block, he saw long stretches of shoveled sidewalks. The good people of Chicago had been busy while he'd been losing himself in the feel of Finn's lips against his as he'd always dreamed. He pushed down a sigh, not wanting her to guess how reluctant he was to give up her company.

"Give me a second to get my things together and I'll get gone."

She was slow to turn from the window, and when she did, her mouth was turned down at the corners in a frown. "Okay."

He ducked into Josie's room and pulled off his borrowed clothes. His own jeans had dried stiff after he'd submerged them in snow, and his henley had definitely seen cleaner days, but they'd work to get him back home.

He emerged dressed like himself again and packed up the few items he'd left scattered on the table. Normally he took more care when he stowed his laptop and notes, but a voice in his brain was shouting that the sooner he got out of there, the less likely he was to say or do something stupid.

Finn remained motionless as he crossed the room to slide on his coat. Even though he was doing his best to exit without embarrassing himself, "something stupid" was brewing on the tip of his tongue. He could offer her his phone number or ask to see her again. He could thank her for providing evidence that every so often, good things did come his way.

He couldn't force any of the words past his tongue though. He was lucky to have gotten the chance to set things right with her and shake the Etch A Sketch clean. Asking for anything else was asking to be disappointed all over again.

He hiked his bag up his shoulder. "Okay then. Thank you for everything. The food, the shelter." The forgiveness. "See you around maybe."

Although it killed him to do it, he turned away from her and put his hand on the knob.

"Or you could stay."

He pivoted slowly, certain his ears had tricked him. "What?"

She still hovered by the window, but she lifted her chin to meet his gaze with something like defiance. "Stay, Tom. You should stay."

She wanted him. She was choosing this. The blood leaped in his veins, and he dropped his bag by the door and stalked across the room to cradle her face in his hands. "Christ, I'm glad you asked."

He kissed her then, without finesse or even tenderness, just an onslaught of lips and tongue against hers, telling her without words that he wanted her, had wanted her forever, and he couldn't wait another second to make her his.

She wrapped a hand around his neck and kissed him back, meeting his ferocity with her own. Her fingers clawed at his coat before working their way inside and over his shoulders to push it off his body. They left it in a puddle of puffy blue fabric at their feet, and he walked her backward toward her bedroom, never breaking their kiss.

At the foot of her bed, she pulled away to study him. Her accelerated breathing stretched the material of her shirt across her breasts, where he could see the points of her nipples. Everything in him screamed to touch, to taste, but he managed to leash his desire.

"Finn, we don't have to do anything here. We can—"

"Don't you dare. I want it all. *Everything.*" Her voice was savage, and blood surged to his cock at the sound of it.

Time to drop the leash.

"Shirt off," he ordered, and she complied instantly. "Those too." He pointed to her leggings.

She tugged them off along with her underwear and tossed them to the side. And then Finn Carey was standing in front of him, naked, nervous, and more beautiful than he could've imagined, and *oh*, had he imagined.

She blushed, and he realized he'd spoken his thoughts out loud. But if anything, it chased the nerves from her face, and despite the flame in her cheeks, she put a hand on her cocked hip.

"Now you. Off."

She waved a finger from his head to his toes, like a queen commanding a servant, and he did as instructed, shedding all the material that was keeping them from being skin-to-skin. Her tongue poked over the edge of her top lip as her avid gaze followed the now-bare path she'd sketched with her finger. He felt the weight of her eyes on his skin like a physical touch, and he couldn't help but grin.

"Looks like I'm not getting out of here with my virtue intact after all." How he had the wherewithal to joke, he didn't know, what with there being no blood left in his head.

He stepped closer and settled his hands around her waist, guiding her to sit on the side of the bed. Then he bent and kissed his way down her body, starting at her lips and moving down to her neck, then to each of her small, perfect breasts until she was gasping and tugging at his hair.

He knelt and looked up at her, this woman who'd been the central fantasy for the bulk of his fantasy-having life. Her black hair was a tangle down her back, her eyes were dreamy, and her mouth was soft and open. Because of him.

Keeping his eyes locked on hers, he stroked a thumb down the wet center of her. "What do you like?"

Nothing but a gasp spilled from her pink mouth, so he repeated the motion.

"Slow? Fast? Hard? Gentle? Tell me what you like, Finn."

She released a shuddery breath. "You. I like *you* touching me, I don't care how. Please—"

It was the permission he was looking for. He put a hand on her solar plexus and pushed her back on the bed, then settled between her legs. Every part of her was pretty, and as he put his mouth and then his tongue on her and then inside her, every part of him was grateful for it.

"Oh God, Tom." She gasped when he added his fingers to the mix, and then her words dissolved into a chant of "yes" and "there" and "more" until she pulsed and cried out and arched off the bed.

He could still feel little aftershocks quivering across her skin when she propped herself up on one elbow and pointed to her bedside table. "Condom. Drawer. Now," she panted.

He hadn't expected to live a blessed enough life to hear Finn Carey issuing one-word commands for him to fuck her, and in the time it took him to yank the drawer open and sheath himself, she'd moved to the center of the bed. He joined her and fell into the cradle of her arms, the vee of her legs. She leaned up to kiss him, sinking her teeth into his lower lip when he didn't push inside her fast enough.

"Fuck, Finn, so good. You feel so good," he ground out, and as he started to move, she rolled her hips to meet him.

He hitched her leg around his hip and stroked into the heat of her, harder, faster, until she was shivering and panting and calling his name. She slipped a hand between their bodies, and he felt her shatter for the second time. His breathing stuttered into gasps, and he followed her over the edge, his face pressed to her neck, his lips seeking her sweet skin, feeling like they'd found their home.

THIRTEEN

Was she dead? Had Tom fucked her to paradise?

No. In paradise, your arm probably didn't fall asleep when it ended up underneath your partner as he drifted off after making your whole body ring like a bell.

Pins and needles were worth it though. Tom's hair was soft against her skin, and his heavy arm curled around her waist. She felt warm and content in a way she hadn't... well, ever, maybe. Thank God she'd summoned every scrap of her courage and asked him to stay.

Tom chose that moment to open his eyes, but she wasn't embarrassed to be caught studying his sleepy face, not when it caused him to unfurl that slow, sweet smile.

"Your dimples, Tom. How can anybody resist those dimples?" She brushed a fingertip gently across one, which deepened as his smile grew.

"I'm just glad they finally worked on you."

Boy, had they. Every woman should experience the intensity of Tom Castle focusing on her and her only, applying his body solely for her pleasure. She shivered at the memory of his eyes locking on hers as he slid into her, filling her completely.

He rolled and sat up, and she watched transfixed as the muscles along his lean torso bunched and shifted.

"Yum." She stroked a hand down his stomach and was delighted when his mouth fell open and his eyelids fluttered. "Can you serve me dinner on these abs tonight?"

"Perv." He said it so affectionately that she laughed. Then he yawned, stretched, and reclined back on the bed. "Let's spend the day like this. Monday too. Call in to work. Play hooky with me. I'll read you the rest of *The Color of Magic* while we're both naked."

She didn't have to give it a second thought. Grabbing her shirt from the floor, she darted to the kitchen where she'd left her phone and crawled back into bed. While she'd been gone, Tom had stretched himself out on his back, his arms behind his head in a classic satisfied-male pose.

She opened her email and tapped out a quick message to her boss: *Not feeling so hot. Okay if I take a sick day tomorrow? When I'm back, we can go over the focus group questions I emailed last week.*

"I'm ahead of my project deadline, so he won't care if I use one of my sick days," she said. "And Josie won't be home until tomorrow night, so it's only us for the next thirty hours."

He ran his hot gaze down her body. "What *am* I going to do with you?"

"Not sure. Usually people come to me for market research and audience surveys. This is a new situation." New, unexpected, and utterly thrilling.

He tilted his head. "Okay then. Show me how you survey an audience."

Oooh, she loved that lazy tone of command. And if he wanted to play, she could play. She stretched to grab the Bullet Journal, a pen, and a hair elastic from her bedside table, then settled cross-legged while Tom pulled himself into a sitting position, covered only by a sheet.

"All right, Mr. Castle." She coiled her hair into a quick bun on top of her head and adopted the crisp focus group voice that she used to command the attention of the room. "I understand you want some market research conducted. As our sample size is quite small, you'll forgive me if I focus my questions on you."

"I'm all yours."

The warmth in his voice momentarily threw her out of the role. He sounded so sincere that she felt for a second as if it were actually true, that he *was* pledging his devotion. Which was ridiculous; this was a crazy, one-off weekend that flew in the face of her orderly life. But while she was spending one more day terrifying herself with spontaneous decisions, she might as well run at them full speed. She continued in her crisp voice.

"First question: On a scale of one to ten, how satisfied are you by your recent experience with the product?"

"Is your pussy the product?"

His coarse words sent a wicked thrill through her, and she flushed. "Y-yes."

"Ten," he growled.

She jotted the number down, if only to escape the intensity of his gaze. "And how likely are you to use the product again? On a scale from one to ten."

"Eleven."

She pursed her lips to keep from laughing. "So I, ah, take it you don't view this as a single-use product?"

He raised his brows. "Oh, I think there's fun to be had with single-use too."

Then, to her dismay and delight, he slipped his hand under the blanket and started to move it up and down his cock.

"N-no, sir, the question referred to—"

"I know what it referred to, Ms. Carey. Please ask the next question."

His hand kept working under the sheet, and Finn felt an answering pulse between her legs.

She cleared her throat and clung to her journal. "Question four: How likely are you to recommend the product to others?"

"Someone else? One to ten?"

She nodded, and possessiveness flared in his eyes.

"Zero. Negative fifty. An irrational number's worth of no."

She had to swallow a few times before she found her voice. "Question five: Do you have suggestions for ways to improve the product that we can pass along to our designers?"

The muscles in his arms tensed as he worked himself, and when he spoke again, his voice held a similar note of tension. "Not sure. I might need another demonstration."

"Oh fuck," she groaned, heedlessly tossing her journal to the floor.

In one smooth movement, she peeled off her shirt and stretched to grab another condom from the drawer. Then she yanked the sheet back to reveal the whole, lovely length of him straining toward her.

He hissed as she rolled on the condom and straddled his lap, guiding his dick where she needed it most. She set the pace, a languid rocking motion that created friction in all the best places. He reached up to free her hair, and it slipped down to brush against his shoulders as she ground against him. He grabbed a fistful with one hand and gripped her hip with the other, positioning her where he wanted so he could reach her breasts with his mouth. Finn thought she might lose her mind as he took care to torture each nipple with licks and bites. Faster than she would've thought possible, she felt the pressure build in her again, and she increased her pace until she hovered on the brink.

"I'm going to... Oh Tom, God, I'm so close," she gasped.

"Then come for me." He sucked her nipple into his mouth and pressed his thumb to her clit, and she shattered. Moments later so did he, and together they answered question five: nothing could improve that user experience.

FOURTEEN

Had there been a time when Tom hadn't liked doing the dishes?

Possibly. But that had been before he'd stood in Finn's kitchen with the weak Monday morning sunshine hitting his shoulders as he kissed her senseless against the sink while the spray from the water misted over both of them.

"You should always wash dishes shirtless," she murmured against his lips.

"And you shouldn't be allowed to wear pants when you're indoors."

His hands moved down to cup her ass, which was bare but for the tiny scrap of lace and cotton she called panties. Her hair was mussed from his fingers and her lips plump from his kisses. He'd never seen her look so undone, and he wanted to lap up every bit of the dishevelment he'd caused by making love to her all day yesterday.

She hooked a heel around his calf, giving him better access to her sweet center. "Thank God for electricity and heat. I'll never take my ability to go pantsless for granted again."

He bent his head and kissed her. She was in his veins now. Her taste, her smell, her laugh. He'd imagined it for years, and the reality had been even more intoxicating.

He slid his fingers under the edge of the material keeping him from where he most wanted to be, and Finn's breathing hitched. He was so focused on finding her wet heat that he didn't hear the key rattling in the front door or the squeak of the hinges as it opened.

"Hi, babycakes, what's shaking? I caught an earlier flight, so— Oh my God, I'm so sorry!" Tom and Finn both froze as the redhead in the doorway shrieked and covered her eyes. "I didn't know you had company!"

For a moment, the only sound in the apartment was the water splashing in the sink as Tom worked to catch up with what was happening. It appeared that Josie was home, and she'd caught him rounding third base with her roommate.

Correction: her *mortified* roommate. Finn jumped away from him, her face going eight shades of red as she tugged on the hem of her shirt.

"Josie! I didn't expect you back so soon!"

"Obviously n— *Tom?*" Josie's eyes narrowed as she got a good look at who her roommate had been kissing. The shock on her face turned to confusion. "I don't understand. What's he still doing here?"

Josie's confusion confused Tom. "Finn, didn't you tell her?"

"That she hooked up with the guy I brought home from the bar on Wednesday?" Josie gave a disbelieving laugh. "I'd definitely remember if she had."

Finn gestured helplessly between her and Tom. "No, see, he's just..."

Her voice trailed off, and the warm glow inside Tom started to fade.

"I'm just *what*?"

"Real classy, Finn." Josie stomped through the kitchen toward her room, her suitcase clattering along behind her.

Finn shot him a stricken glance before hustling after her roommate. "There was nothing to tell! He's just somebody I knew from high school, and he got stuck here during the blizzard when—"

Finn followed Josie into the bedroom, shutting the door behind her. Tom could hear the rise and fall of their voices, but he didn't need to stick around for specifics. Finn had used the word *just* to describe him a few too many times, and even if she was trying to keep peace with her roommate, she'd had days and days to tell Josie that he was still in their apartment. She simply hadn't bothered. The old wound opened up in his chest as he realized that yet again, Beauty wasn't choosing Brains; she'd only been slumming it for the weekend.

Most of his belongings were already tucked into the bag he'd dropped by the front door yesterday, so he ducked into Finn's room to finish dressing. Seconds after he stepped into the hallway wearing his own clothes, Josie burst out of her bedroom and stopped short, a sneer spreading across her face.

"Well, this has been enlightening. I'm going to shower the airplane off me while you two carry on with your not-at-all-weird encounter." She threw a glance at Finn, who'd followed her out of the bedroom. "But if I were you, I'd be damn careful about what I texted him. You never know when he might be tempted to share again."

All the breath left Tom's body as Josie pushed past

him to the bathroom, and he spun around to face Finn, who sagged against the doorframe, her face ashen.

"You told her?" He gripped his hair, barely able to speak for the tightness in his throat. "Jesus *Christ*, I thought we covered this."

"I didn't expect her back so soon," she whispered. "I didn't think I'd have to explain things with you still here."

She'd expected him to leave. She'd wanted him gone. The realization shouldn't have blindsided him, but it did. His hurt howled to be set free, and he bit out, "So sorry to have overstayed my welcome."

"It's not that!" she cried, all traces of that morning's carefree joy drained and gone. "It's a big adjustment, okay? To go from thinking of you as the guy who humiliated me in front of the whole class to"—she waved a hand in his direction—"*this.*"

"This" told him nothing. He had no idea what "this" meant to Finn. He waited for her to clarify, but she fixed her eyes on the ground, letting her hair obscure her features. And suddenly he was right back where he used to be: the guy pining for the girl who'd never be his. He thought they'd put the past to bed, literally, but he'd clearly been wrong. The optimism that had filled the indentation in his heart drained away, leaving it hollow and aching again.

He paced to the kitchen and wrapped his hands around the back of a chair, willing it to anchor him to the spot so he could say what he needed to say. "Your text message, when you told me you wanted somebody who sees you?" He met her eyes and willed himself not to soften at the tears he saw there. "That's me, Finn. It's always been me, and all I've ever wanted is the same thing in return. This weekend, I thought we were finally getting there, together. But I was wrong. You still don't believe me."

The painful truth of those last five words seared him, as did Finn's rapid breathing. "I *do*. I was just trying to explain our history to Josie."

"Our history." He gave a snide laugh, reached into his pocket, and tossed his phone on the kitchen table, where it skidded to a stop in front of her. "There you go. Eight one six three nine three. Type it in and scroll through everything. Make sure I didn't collect any personal information on you while I was here, given our *history* and all."

She crossed her arms over her midsection and wrapped her trembling hands around her elbows. "No, Tom. I don't need to—"

He snatched the phone from the table and unlocked it himself. He was acting like the asshole she'd always thought he was, and he couldn't bring himself to stop.

"No texts since I don't have your number, but you can't be too careful around me, can you?" The words hurt to speak, but he pushed them out anyway, low and harsh. He opened his photo gallery with a furious jab of his finger, turning the screen toward her. "Here. See? Awful stuff."

He selected an image and started scrolling one by one.

A shot of him and his buddy Sam at the bar on Wednesday night.

A shot of Finn's street on Thursday evening, the snowbanks crawling up the sides of the building opposite her apartment.

A shot of flakes drifting past the streetlight on her corner.

A shot of Finn, wrapped in a blanket up to her ears on

Saturday night during the power outage, peering out the window and outlined in silvery moonlight.

"Happy?"

She shook her head. "No, I—"

His hand clenched around his phone. "Fine, then how about this?" With a series of taps, he deleted all the photos he'd taken that weekend. They vanished with a *whoosh*, and fuck, if only he could empty his own memories as easily. She reached a hand out, maybe to stop him, maybe to encourage him to hurry out the door. He was too tired to care anymore.

"Tom, wait. Please listen."

"No. I'm done." He tugged on his coat and shouldered his bag, ready to put Finn behind him. Again. "Have a nice life, Huck."

He stepped through the door and let it fall shut behind him with a heavy slam, taking grim satisfaction that at least this time *he* was the one choosing to walk away.

FIFTEEN

Finn lasted fifteen whole seconds after Tom's devastating exit before the tears started.

Somehow, through a few careless words, her whole beautiful weekend had collapsed. She'd been too flustered by Josie's anger and her own unexpected emotional one-eighty to find a way to make him listen.

The tears came harder and harder, and the next thing she knew, Josie was there, damp from the shower, wrapping an arm around her shoulder and guiding her to the couch.

"Sit." She pushed Finn down onto the cushions and draped a blanket around her. She disappeared briefly and returned with a glass of water, a box of Kleenex, and a pair of leggings. "Put some pants on so we can talk."

Finn offered a soggy laugh at her roommate's take-no-shit tone. "Yes, ma'am." She pulled on the leggings, then sat back down to blow her nose and mop her face.

After a moment, Josie sighed. "So I guess I didn't handle that very well."

"Ya think?" Finn's voice was scratchy from crying.

"But can you blame me? He was straight, single, and beautiful, and *I* brought him home. How often do I hit the trifecta?" Her roommate tipped forward to wrap her hair in a towel-turban, craning her neck to peer up at Finn. "Except for your brother, of course."

"Please don't refer to Jake as beautiful when I'm around." Any mild amusement she felt over Josie's futile crush on her workaholic brother was swept up in another small sob. "I don't know what happened."

Josie tucked one leg underneath her and turned to face Finn. "Um, I happened. You clearly had some kind of major personal revelation this weekend, and then I came home and acted like a jealous bitch because..." She gestured helplessly. "I mean, I spent all weekend thinking about Tom! He's hot. And he seemed nice."

"He is. And he is," Finn said dully, her stomach roiling at the memory of the fight leaving Tom's eyes. She could actually pinpoint the precise moment that he gave up on her. "He looked so *broken* when he left."

"I'm sorry. I shouldn't have gotten involved. You told me you believed he didn't do it, and then I went and let my redhead out."

Act, then think. It's how Josie always operated. Finn had borrowed a page from that playbook during the past few days, and look where it had gotten her. "It's my fault too," she said, wiping her eyes on the sleeve of her sweatshirt. "I didn't tell you he'd stayed the weekend. And then I didn't stand up for him. I made him feel unimportant when actually he's so, so important." Her head was too heavy for her neck to support, so she dropped it on Josie's robe-covered shoulder.

Josie smoothed Finn's hair back from her forehead. "It's not totally your fault. You unexpectedly reconnected with someone you used to care about. It sounds like it got really intense, really fast, and you probably didn't know how to handle it because it didn't fit into the goals in your Bullet Journal. Then I came home and made things worse. Your guy left, and you forgot how pants work. The end."

"That's... actually pretty much it." Finn snuffled. "I will say you got him right in his most vulnerable spot."

Josie shrugged, the motion jostling Finn's head. "That seems to be my specialty."

Finn sat up and took one more swipe at her wet eyes. "Is your other specialty fixing things after you and I worked together to screw things up for me with the guy you brought home?"

Josie slapped her hands on her thighs and then stood. "Absolutely not. My specialty is pouring the wine until you forget about your woes. I take it you were planning to stay home from work today?"

Finn nodded. "We were going to—"

Her roommate held up a hand. "I know what you were planning to do. I saw those abs." She tapped out a quick text message, then looked up with a raised eyebrow. "The only acceptable alternative is getting good and day drunk. Richard's on the way."

Three hours later, Finn was impervious to pain.

"*That* guy wore my pants?" Richard grabbed the laptop from her and held it to his nose, barely avoiding dribbling wine on the keyboard.

"Yep," she said, grabbing his glass and stealing a sip for herself when she found her own empty. "And I swear to God, if you accidentally like a single thing on his timeline from my account, I will murder you."

"Girl, you think I don't know how to social media

stalk?" Richard snatched his glass back and took a closer look at the screen. "It's actually a miracle that Calamity Josie found him without me around to nudge her away from the marrieds and the Marys."

Josie smacked Richard's arm and swiped the laptop, scrolling on Tom's Insta until she found a shot of the man in question in swim trunks at Oak Street Beach. "Oh my God. Those arms."

"He looked amaaaaazing in Richard's shirts." Finn had reached the swoony, dreamy stage of drunkenness where everything was rosy around the edges. "He also looked amazing *out* of Richard's shirts."

"Staaahp. You're making us all jealous." Josie returned with a fresh bottle of wine to top off everyone's glasses.

"Not me." Richard raised his newly full glass in a salute. "I proposed to Byron last night. We're getting married!"

Finn shrieked, and Josie shoved the laptop at her so she could wrap Richard into a hug. "Congratulations! Let me be your ring bearer? Please please please?"

Richard ruffled Josie's curls. "You can absolutely carry a white satin pillow down the aisle. But I now speak from a place of authority as a happily settled man. That means you all have to listen."

He paused to take a long gulp from his glass, and Finn leaned forward so she wouldn't miss a word. But she misjudged her wine-enhanced ability to keep her balance and ended up toppling sideways, taking her full glass with her. Normally she'd freak over the stain seeping into her sweatshirt, but today she couldn't bring herself to care. Too bad she was drinking merlot and not chardonnay.

"Finn, my dear, the thing you have to understand is

—" Richard began, only to be interrupted by a knock on the door.

Finn's soggy, foolish heart lurched. Tom had come back. She'd get the chance to apologize. They could try again. Well, *again* again.

"Finn! Are you here?"

Everything in her wilted. She knew that voice, and it didn't belong to the man she most wanted to see. Still, its owner would probably remove the screws on the hinges if she didn't let him in pronto, so she rolled her boneless self off the couch and slouched to the door.

"Jake," she muttered. "Why aren't you at work? Is it a national holiday? Christmas was last month."

Her corporate-polish brother looked ragged round the edges, his black hair spiked in tufts around his head. "You weren't. Answering. Your phone," he ground out. "We discussed this."

He pointed an accusing finger at her, but she batted it away.

"*Pssht*. I turned off my phone. Big protective brother isn't the boss of me."

Jake's nose twitched. "Are you *drunk*?"

A noise inside the apartment made them both turn to see Josie's and Richard's heads pop over the back of the couch like a pair of lemurs.

"Looking gooooooood, Jake! My replacement trifecta!" Josie accompanied her happy shout with a salute from her half-full wineglass.

In response, Jake plowed his fingers through his hair, which explained its current state of dishevelment, and visibly counted to five before turning to her. "Grab your coat."

BY HER THIRD cup of coffee, Finn forgave her brother for kidnapping her. Mostly.

"Everything was fine," she grumbled. "I was working through some things."

"You were drunk and wallowing," he corrected.

"Po-*tay*-to, po-*tah*-to. You could have at least let me change into something decent."

She gestured angrily at her wine-stained sweatshirt, but their sibling standoff was interrupted when the waitress buzzed by their table yet again to make sure Jake didn't need anything, then almost tripped as she kept her eyes glued on him while she backed away. As usual, her handsome brother was impervious, his gaze on some important email or other on his phone.

"You can go back to the office now. I'm fine."

He set his phone down and hit her with his best all-business stare. "Are you? Because I'm not quite sure why you're in knots over your high school bully."

A wave of protectiveness surged inside her. "I told you I got it wrong. He wasn't the bad guy in all that."

"Okay. But explain the 'in knots' part."

She dragged a fork through the remains of her breakfast-for-late-lunch pancakes. "I think..." Time for confession. "I think the reason I got so mad and stayed mad for so long was that deep down, I liked Tom. I *more* than liked him, even when I was with Dylan. Dylan *was* the high school bully, by the way."

Jake grimaced. "I never liked that guy."

"A letterman jacket is a powerful aphrodisiac for sixteen-year-old girls."

"Oh, I'm painfully aware," he said wryly.

She flashed a quick smile at her brother, who'd been too busy busting his ass making money in high school to mess around with sports. Then she took a deep breath and confronted a truth she'd kept tucked away for years.

"I used to be so relieved when Tom would break up with whatever girl he was seeing, even though it was hypocritical as hell since I was with Dylan the whole time. When he posted those horrible things, I guess it felt easier to never speak to him again instead of asking myself why it hurt so much." She shifted uncomfortably on the bench seat, not wanting to meet Jake's steady brown eyes. "And then eight years later, he magically turned up in my apartment, and it was like I had the chance to work through all of it and maybe have a..."

"A happy ending?" Jake finished her thought.

She flushed and looked up. "Yeah. I thought maybe we could have a happy ending."

"And now you can't?"

Could they? Could she fix what she'd done, undo the hurt she'd caused?

"I don't know."

"Well, don't you think you should at least try?"

Dammit. She hated when Jake was right. Her only choice was to change the subject in the most obnoxious way possible. "So *you're* still single, right? I don't suppose you finally want to take Josie on a date?"

He scoffed and reached for his all-important phone. "She's busting my chops. Josie doesn't actually want to go out with me."

"Um, everybody wants to go out with you. Our Uber driver wanted to go out with you."

He looked up from his phone, startled. "She did not."

"She followed us to the door of the restaurant and

stared at your ass the whole time. And she double-parked to do it!"

He waved a dismissive hand at her. "I'll have time for that later. After I—"

"—make partner at your big, important accounting firm," she finished for him. "I know, I know."

They both fell silent, and Finn knew he was thinking about his eternal quest to sock away enough money so she and her mom would never have to lose sleep over it again, even though she was an employed adult and their mother had moved downstate to marry a nice man who owned a hardware store.

"I'm so proud of everything you've accomplished," she said quietly. "But I also worry about you."

The edges of his lips lifted. "I know. Same way I worry about you. Now," he said, breaking their serious moment, "before I head back to the office, let's discuss the best groveling techniques."

SIXTEEN

"Oh good, you're here."

Tom looked up from his laptop with a glare that he quickly wiped from his face. "Dr. Chadhoury. Hi."

The newest member of his dissertation committee entered his tiny office, which would be cramped even if it were only him occupying the space. Too bad he actually shared it with three other graduate students, like a veal.

"I didn't think I'd find you here. Aren't Mondays your off-campus writing days?" she asked.

He forced a polite smile. "I was anxious for a change of scenery after being cooped up."

Lies. In actuality, he couldn't fathom being alone with his thoughts, so he'd come straight to campus, not even stopping by his apartment to shower or change. Then he'd driven away his officemates one by one with his poisonous mood. *Hello, thoughts. I'm still alone with you, I see.*

"Well, good. I got your message that you couldn't read some of my notes, so I stopped by to interpret."

Her notes. The notes that Finn had read aloud.

Even conjuring her name in his mind shot a dart of

pain into his heart. He'd come so close to capturing joy and holding it in his hands, only to see it slip away because... what, he couldn't escape his past? Couldn't summon the strength to fight for his future?

"Tom?"

The voice jostled him out of his reverie, and he realized he was staring into the middle distance while a senior member of the economics faculty waited for him to get his shit together.

"Sorry." He dragged a hand down his face. "I... it's in this stack somewhere. I think." He pointed at the pile of five-inch binders on his desk. His mind was too jumbled to figure out where he'd stashed her draft a few hours ago.

The tall woman shrugged and adjusted her red silk sari, likely used to disorganized academics. "No worries. I'll see if I scanned a copy before returning it to you." Then she looked at him again. "Everything all right, Thomas? You seem distracted."

He offered her a weak smile. "Yes. Well, no. But it will be."

Her answering smile was full of understanding. "Good. It wouldn't be graduate school if everything wasn't bleak for a bit."

She excused herself, and Tom was alone once again. He still had a mountain of papers to grade, and he really did need to figure out what the hell Dr. Chadhoury had meant to recommend in her notes. But all he could bring himself to do was glare at the industrial beige wall in front of his desk and feel sorry for himself.

Would every little thing remind him of Finn until the end of his days? Or would this current pain eventually fade? And which fate was worse, the pain or the forgetting?

He dropped his head to his desk. Maybe he ought to head home after all. He was only being productive at splashing his emotional mess all over the workplace. And then, maybe tomorrow, he'd go back to Finn's apartment and camp out in her hallway until she was willing to—

"Tom."

He lifted his head, then bolted upright. "Finn!"

Shock kept him from coherent speech, and she took a tentative step into the small room.

"I wasn't sure where to find you, so I came to campus and kept asking and asking until I found your department."

As the surprise of Finn appearing in his doorway wore off, he became aware that she didn't look like her usual immaculate self. Her right knee poked through a large hole in her leggings, and her sweatshirt had a blotchy red stain down the front. She looked hassled and bedraggled and absolutely perfect.

He cleared his throat and did his level best to tamp down his hope. "What, no preprinted campus map? No organized list of questions?"

She looked down at herself and shook her head in bemusement. "I didn't want to wait. Or to plan. I had to find you." She took a deep breath. "I'm here to grovel."

Warmth spread through him, even before she'd finished speaking, and all he wanted to do was scoop her up and never let her go. "That's funny." He kept his voice casual. "I was thinking about heading your way after class tomorrow to give you a chance to do exactly that."

"You were?" Her surprised smile was the best balm in the world for his aching heart.

"I was. And then after you groveled, I was going to make you another omelet."

"Oh my. How generous." Her lips twitched.

"Well, I'm really good at it. I'd hate for you to miss out." He folded his arms over his chest. "Go on then. Get your grovel on."

His heart rattled in his chest as she shifted from foot to foot, wringing her hands. The silence stretched until he burst into laughter.

"You have no idea how to do this, do you? Have you never groveled in your life?"

"No!" She flung her arms into the air. "Okay, how about this? I'm sorry. Please give me another chance?"

He waved a hand for her to continue. "What are you sorry for? Please be specific. Pretend you're reading a list from your journal."

"God, where to start?" She took a deep breath, and he watched the tension leave her body as the words poured out of her. "I believe you. I'm sorry I made you think for even a second this morning that I didn't. And I should've believed that it wasn't you who posted those things about me from the very beginning. I'm sorry I didn't strip you out of your clothes today so you could finish reading *The Color of Magic* to me naked."

As the blissfully unaware Finn spoke, Dr. Chadhoury appeared in the doorway, a stack of papers in her hand and a startled look on her face.

"I'm sorry for not telling Josie immediately that you were stuck in the apartment with me." She took a step toward him. "I'm sorry that I made it sound like what we shared this weekend was anything but special and perfect and by far the best sex I've ever had. I'm sorry we wasted all this time by being apart."

The thought of stopping Finn's words physically pained him, but for the sake of his dignity, he might have to. Thankfully, Dr. Chadhoury's face relaxed into a smile, and she gave him a thumbs-up as she backed out the office, easing the door shut behind her. He'd clearly made the correct choice in his replacement committee member.

Finn barreled on, her voice gaining strength. "I'm sorry I didn't physically throw myself in front of my apartment door to keep you from leaving this morning. I'm sorry I ever spent even one minute as Dylan's girlfriend when you were right in front of me the whole time with your good heart and your quick mind and your beautiful mouth. I'm sorry—"

Tom had heard enough. He crossed the rest of the distance between them and wrapped his arms around her. "Figures you'd be an overachiever even when groveling." Then he pulled her close and kissed her, feeling like the luckiest man alive as those sweet lips opened for him and her hands slid around his waist and grabbed fistfuls of his shirt.

They were both breathing hard when he pulled back far enough to make his own confession. "When we were kids, I hoped without hope that someday I'd get lucky and you'd choose me. And after this weekend..."

A smile trembled on her lips. "After this weekend?"

He kissed her again. "Let's just say I'm optimistic."

EPILOGUE

Two months later

"It's finished."

Tom slumped in the doorway of the bedroom, dark circles under his eyes and curly hair mussed from distracted tousling during his epic dissertation editing session at the kitchen table. Finn flipped back the covers on his side of the bed and patted the empty space next to her. "Every last edit?"

"Every last edit." He slid between the sheets and leaned back against the headboard with a sigh, rubbing his eyes. The sun had set hours ago, and the bedroom was dark but for the bedside lamp.

"How long before I'm calling you Dr. Castle?" She twined her fingers with his, and he cracked open one tawny eye to shoot her a cocky, if tired, grin.

"You can call me that right now if you want, Ms. Carey."

She snapped her Bullet Journal shut and smacked it lightly against his thigh. "Not yet. You have to earn that privilege."

"Then let's hope my dissertation defense goes well next month." The lines around his mouth had grown more pronounced as they'd entered March and the date for him to appear before the committee to answer their probing questions loomed ever closer. Wanting to ease the signs of weariness that dragged him down, Finn leaned forward to kiss first one corner of his mouth and then the other. In truth, what he needed was a straight twelve hours of sleep, but his restless brain rarely allowed that to happen.

"Of course it will." She burrowed her head into the crook of his neck. "You're brilliant, and you've been working nonstop for weeks. You're going to walk in and use your Tom Castle charm to own that room."

His arm snaked around her waist, and he pulled her tightly against him in a one-armed hug, but Finn wanted more than that. She'd been sound asleep when he'd called it quits the past three nights, which was three nights too many to go without kissing him all over. She sat up to put the Bullet Journal on her bedside table, but he laid his hand on the red Moleskine cover still resting on his thigh. "May I?"

She raised her brows but nodded, not sure why he'd be interested in her list of tasks for the upcoming week when they could instead be getting up to far more exciting things. But he surprised her by opening the book to an empty page, picking up her pen, and studying her with a glint in his eyes that ignited a hot spark in her stomach. Something was brewing in his brain, and her gut told her it was important.

"I have some survey questions for you, Ms. Carey."

Although his businesslike tone was at odds with his threadbare Cubs T-shirt, she nodded gravely. "Survey questions? What are you researching?"

He tapped one impatient finger on the journal cover and shot her a long look. "I'm asking the questions, ma'am."

Oooh, she loved that bossy tone, but she bit her lip against the smile that threatened and nodded for him to continue.

He tapped the tip of the pen against the page. "To begin, on a scale of one to ten, how satisfied are you with your current romantic relationship?"

"Hmm." She tipped her head back and pretended to think. "Well, my boyfriend's been pretty distracted with his dissertation, and last week I caught him microwaving coffee that had gotten cold instead of making a new pot."

"Mmm-hmm, okay. So his kitchen skills could be improved." Tom ran his finger down the page as if checking something off a list. "Does he have any other areas that need attention?"

Finn's smile softened as she considered the delight this man brought to her life every day. "Let's see... he makes me laugh and listens when I tell him about my day and plays with my hair and looks good in my fuzzy socks. I can't think of a single thing I'd change."

The corner of Tom's mouth kicked up. "So on a satisfaction scale of one to ten..."

"Nine point nine," she said firmly. "He loses point one for the coffee thing. I mean, we're not animals."

"Okay, good." Tom pretended to jot that down and then paused a beat before asking, "And how likely are you to remain in this relationship for the foreseeable future?"

Her cheeks heated as Tom's gaze remained on the page in front of him. Although they'd spent the bulk of their free time together since that most fortuitous blizzard, they rarely talked about the future. The closest they came was agreeing on a restaurant to try that weekend or daydreaming about chucking it all and moving somewhere tropical to escape the grueling Chicago winters.

"Scale of one to ten?" She was stalling, unsure if she was brave enough to give him the answer that slammed against her rib cage and begged to be let loose.

Tom looked up. "One to ten." His voice was rough, his eyes burning into hers, and Finn realized that her answer *mattered*.

She drew a deep breath, pushed the air out of her lungs, and said, "Ten."

Tom's eyes brightened even more at her response. "And how likely is that response to change if your boyfriend joins the new economic think tank that's opening its doors in Chicago this summer?"

She gasped. "Really? You finally accepted one of your job offers?"

He looked at her sternly. "Do I need to remind you again who's asking the questions?"

She looked down in mock meekness, although inside she was doing flips. "Very sorry, sir. A job at an ethical investing nonprofit gets an enthusiastic ten. And if it makes my boyfriend happy, then I'm happy."

"Excellent." Tom nodded, then visibly tensed as he stared hard at the open journal page in front of him. "Last question. On a scale of one to ten, with one being 'I am in a medically induced coma' and ten being 'I am running through the wall in a panic like the Kool-Aid Man,' how much would it freak you out if your boyfriend told you he loved you?"

Finn's throat closed up so tightly that she couldn't push any words out, and her silence finally pulled Tom's eyes from the page to meet hers. In them, she saw hope and heat and a touch of fear that she wanted to chase away for good.

"Tom, I..." She blinked rapidly as tears started to gather, and Tom gently pressed a thumb to the corner of her lashes.

"Scale of one to ten, Huck," he said gruffly.

"Ten. I mean one." Her voice sounded thick, and her brain stopped processing numbers. "Whichever one gets you to say it to me right now, that's the number I am."

Tom captured her hand with his and pressed a kiss to her palm, where his touch tingled as if this were the first time his skin had met hers.

"I love you, Finn," he said with a twist of his lips that showed off those perfect dimples. "So much. On a scale of one to ten, it's ten million. They haven't invented a Bullet Journal with enough pages to capture all the love in my heart for you."

Finn gave a little sob and moved her hand to his chest, seeking out the steady beat of his heart. "And I love you too, enough to fill ten million journals."

He leaned forward and kissed her softly, thoroughly, leaving her warm and breathless and thrilled down to her toes. "Enough to endure ten million snowed-in weekends with me?"

She twined her arms around his neck. "Enough to eat ten million of your omelets and drink ten million cups of coffee with you and listen to you read me ten million books."

He rolled to his back and carried her with him, stretching them out side by side on the mattress. "The luckiest day of my life was the day I overslept in a strange apartment." He stroked a hand down her hair, and she wriggled even closer to him.

"The luckiest day of *my* life was when you let me grovel to win you back," she said, pressing a kiss to his mouth. "And guess what? Our luck's only going to get better from here."

And then they both stopped talking so she could prove that she was right.

Want to cuddle up with more Tom and Finn?
Head here for a swoony bonus epilogue!
www.sarawhitney.com/heat

*The Tempt Me series continues with **Tempting Taste**. Would you believe that Finn's feisty roommate Josie finds her perfect match in a grumpy baker who'd rather be dipped in acid than carry on a conversation lasting longer than two minutes? Available now!*

Dear reader,

Thank you so much for picking up *Tempting Heat*! Your time and money are precious, and I'm tickled fuchsia that you chose to spend some of both with Tom and Finn.

When my husband and I were in the early stages of dating, we took turns reading out loud to each other. The *Harry Potter* series. *Bridget Jones's Diary*. And yes, *The Color of Magic* by the incomparable Terry Pratchett. It helped the two of us fall in love, and it affirmed that reading would play a central role in our relationship.

Likewise I hope the words you just read made you fall a little in love with Tom and Finn and that you'll continue your journey with the rest of the books in the Tempt Me series. *Tempting Taste*, book two, is Finn's roommate's love story. Josie can be... well, she can be a bit much, honestly. But she's a good person at heart, and you'll swoon as she falls in love with her utterly dreamy polar opposite. *Tempting Taste* is available for purchase now!

If you don't want to miss out on any of my upcoming releases, sales, or giveaways, be sure to sign up for my VIP mailing list: **sarawhitney.com/newsletter**

Stay sassy, and stay in touch!

Sara Whitney

The Tempt Me Series

Tempting Heat
Tempting Taste
Tempting Talk
Tempting Lies

Praise for Sara Whitney

Tempting Taste

"Sara Whitney has pulled together the most fun you'll have in a bakery with this one! I loved the cupcake-baking, cinnamon roll hero who looks like the God of Thunder. Hello to my new book boyfriend." *Christina Hovland, author of the Mile High Matched series*

"Sexy, sassy, and downright delicious! Whitney's pint-sized heroine and strong-but-silent hero make for the perfect pairing. Tempting Taste brims with her trademark wit, humor and warmth." *Kate Bateman, author of This Earl Of Mine*

"A fun, sexy read full of humor and heart." *Sarah Hegger, author of Positively Pippa and Roughing*

Tempting Lies

"Sweet and funny and sexy all at once. I couldn't put this down." *Marianela Aybar, Mari Loves Books Blog*

"This book kept me laughing. I am super excited to check out more books by Sara Whitney." *Stevie, Book Obsessed Reviews*

"The roller-coaster ride the author takes us on getting to their happily ever after left me feeling slightly broken but so happy and hopeful. Even though I've only just closed the cover on this book, I'm already looking forward to what the author has in store for us with the next installment in the series." *Kristen Lewendon, Renaissance Dragon Book Blog*

Tempting Talk

"This story made me laugh, sigh, shout in triumph and blink away tears." *Faith Hart, author of Another Try*

"The interactions are hilarious, while the sparks are flying everywhere. I was all in cover to cover." *Jennifer Pierson, The Power of Three Readers*

"A sweet, witty, and engaging story featuring likable, complex characters." *Laurie, Laurie Reads Romance*

Tempting Heat

"It made my heart squeeze and my cheeks flush. Finn and Tom are 100% guaranteed to make. you. swoon." *Blair Leigh, author of What Comes After*

"A brilliant read. I adored it from beginning to end." *Sandra, Jeanz Book Read & Review*

"The perfect amount of tension, smoldering heat, unexpected twists, and satisfying conclusion." *Sarah, Paranormal Peach Reviews*

ABOUT THE AUTHOR

Sara Whitney writes sassy contemporary romance that's always sunny with a chance of sizzle. An RWA© Golden Heart© award finalist, Sara worked as a print journalist and film critic before she earned her Ph.D. and landed in academia. She's a good pinball player, a great baker, and an expert at shouting her TV opinions to anyone who'll listen. Sara lives in Illinois surrounded by books, cats, and half-empty coffee cups. She loves hearing from readers, so connect with her on social media!

- facebook.com/sarawhitneyauthor
- amazon.com/author/sarawhitney
- instagram.com/sarawhitney_
- bookbub.com/profile/sara-whitney
- goodreads.com/SaraWhitney_
- twitter.com/sarawhitney_